THREAT
OF EXPOSURE
LYNETTE EASON

Special thanks and acknowledgment to Lynette Eason for her contribution to the Texas Ranger Justice miniseries.

Recycling programs
for this product may
not exist in your area.

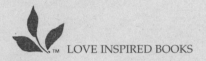 LOVE INSPIRED BOOKS

ISBN-13: 978-0-373-67462-6

THREAT OF EXPOSURE

Copyright © 2011 by Harlequin Books S.A.

www.LoveInspiredBooks.com

Printed in U.S.A.

The powers that be in the Ranger department had sent a lone woman down here to investigate. What were they thinking?

Of course Brock was with her, but still...

Just as he was about to step back inside his own hotel room, Gisella appeared in the doorway next to his. "You all set?" he asked.

She looked up to meet his eyes, and his blood pumped a little faster. She had beautiful, big brown eyes. Eyes that made a man want to act like a brainless sap and get lost in them. He blinked. "You bet." She gave him a funny smile. "You?"

He nodded, then said, "But sleep with your gun close by. These locks are pitiful."

She gave him another soft smile that made his heart do things it hadn't done in a long time. He gulped and ordered himself not to be attracted to her.

It didn't work.

TEXAS RANGER JUSTICE:
Keeping the Lone Star State safe

LYNETTE EASON

grew up in Greenville, South Carolina. Her home church, Northgate Baptist, had a tremendous influence on her during her early years. She credits Christian parents and dedicated Sunday school teachers for her acceptance of Christ at the tender age of eight. Even as a young girl, she knew she wanted her life to reflect the love of Jesus.

Lynette attended the University of South Carolina in Columbia, SC, then moved to Spartanburg, SC, to attend Converse College, where she obtained her master's degree in education. During that time, she met the boy next door, Jack Eason, and married him. Jack is the executive director of the Sound of Light Ministries. Lynette and Jack have two precious children—Lauryn, eight years old, and Will, who is six. She and Jack are members of New Life Baptist Fellowship Church in Boiling Springs, SC, where Jack serves as the worship leader and Lynette teaches Sunday school to the four- and five-year-olds.

Arise, O Lord,
in your anger; rise up against the ra[g]
my enemies. Awake, my God; decree jus[t]
—*Psalms* 7:6

Will,
se of right and wrong.
Lord, stand strong
ate for justice.
and I love you more!

e of
ice.

ONE

DEA agent Brock Martin stared at the man behind the gun. The man who was supposed to be his informant. The man who'd sold accurate information to him over the last year. A man who Brock hadn't come to trust, but *had* come to rely on.

The cold January wind blew across his face, but that wasn't what caused his violent shudder. "What are you doing, Lenny?"

One minute they were talking like always, the next, the weapon had appeared in Lenny's hand almost before Brock could blink. The move had been totally unexpected and Brock drew in a deep breath, ready to draw on all of his hostage negotiation training.

Then Lenny gave a smile that chilled his blood. "I got a better offer from Harry Lowe. He decided you've caused him enough grief and lost profit."

Harry Lowe. A big-time drug dealer along the Mexico-Texas border. Brock had been working this area between Juarez, Mexico, and El Paso, Texas, a long time. But one small slipup and he could die.

Lenny's cold eyes and steady hand holding the weapon said Brock had slipped up.

In a major way.

Dread and fear clawed its way into his chest. He swallowed hard trying to figure out how he'd ended up in this predicament. "Lenny, come on, man, you don't want to do this. Everyone at the station knows I'm meeting with you. And they're waiting for me to get back with whatever you have for me."

A nervous twitch of Lenny's left eye told Brock that it didn't matter. The man's hand trembled as he stared down the barrel.

Right now Lenny was more scared of not doing what Harry Lowe wanted than he was of going to jail for murder.

Not a good situation for Brock.

More fear and no small amount of self-disgust curled through his gut. He'd gotten careless. Now, it seemed it might be his night to die. He'd always wondered how it would happen. How he would go. If he'd be ready.

He wasn't.

But now it seemed in this small church parking lot, hidden in the shadows of the trees, he was going to face his maker.

God, please…

His mind formed the prayer even as he calculated

the odds of successfully jumping Lenny. He realized he would have no chance of tackling the man or reaching for his own weapon, now on the ground to his left, before Lenny pulled the trigger.

So he had to make a choice. Jump Lenny and take his chances or bolt for cover and hope Lenny's aim was off.

Bad odds all around.

Lenny sniffed and aimed the gun point-blank at Brock's head. "Sorry, dude, but a man's gotta do what a…"

"Put the gun down, Lenny!" the voice came from Brock's left behind the trees. Lenny jerked, whipped the gun toward the voice, and pulled the trigger.

Brock darted to the bumper of his vehicle, wishing he hadn't kicked his weapon quite so hard when Lenny had demanded he drop it. It glinted under the streetlamp ten yards away, mocking his incompetence.

Then he heard the pop of another bullet and felt the buzz as it careened past his cheek to plant itself in the asphalt beside him. *God, get me out of this, please. I'm not ready to face You yet.*

Adrenaline pumping, he rolled for cover even as he heard the discharge of another weapon, the howl of pain and the thud of a body hitting the asphalt.

Running footsteps echoed behind him as he lunged for Lenny, who now lay face down, and kicked his gun from his outstretched hand. Brock flipped the man, then planted a knee in his would-be killer's back as he swiped the cuffs from his belt.

Through gritted teeth, Brock muttered, "You're under arrest for the attempted murder of a law enforcement officer. You have the right to remain…" He broke off as a pair of boots stepped into his line of vision.

With Lenny's hands securely fastened behind his back, Brock allowed his eyes to travel north from the boots, up a pair of jean-clad legs to a belt fastened around a slim waist he could probably span with his hands. He let his gaze wander on up to the white shirt with a badge.

A badge with a star inside it. Right over the wearer's heart. She held her weapon ready and steady.

When he finally reached his rescuer's face, he knew in his gut exactly who'd saved his life.

"Hello, Ranger Hernandez." Brock hauled his now-subdued prisoner to his feet and stared at one of the most beautiful women he'd ever seen. Tall, lean and fit, she kept steady brown eyes glued to his. He swiped an arm across his forehead. "I'll say this for you. You have impeccable timing."

Ranger Gisella Hernandez flipped her braid over her shoulder and stared at the man she'd already decided she didn't like very much.

Number one, he'd stood her up.

Number two, he'd met with a known drug runner without any backup.

Number three, he hadn't said "thank you" for her saving his life.

And she was supposed to work with him. As if she needed life to get any more interesting.

Give him a chance, she ordered herself.

She gave her hat a shove back on her head and addressed his timing comment. "You were supposed to meet me over two hours ago. I don't like to be kept waiting."

The man before her blew out a short laugh. "And I don't like to look death in the face. Looks like neither one of us was meant to be happy tonight."

For some reason, that comment amused her. She appreciated the fact that she didn't seem to intimidate him, as her badge seemed to scare off more men than it attracted. Gisella fought to keep the smile from curving her lips, but wasn't sure she succeeded when he raised a knowing brow. She gestured toward Lenny. "How's he?"

Brock shot the man a disgusted frown. "It's a shoulder wound. He'll live." Gisella thought she heard a silent "unfortunately" on the end of that last sentence.

"I wasn't gonna kill you. You got this all wrong," Lenny whined. He looked at Gisella. "I can't believe you shot me."

She turned to the dealer and gave him a stare that

made him cringe. "I wouldn't have given you any warning if I'd had a choice." She looked at Brock. "You were right in my line of fire. I had to do a little maneuvering."

So that was why she'd yelled. Typically, in that kind of volatile situation, a cop shot first, two lethal pops to the chest, and it was over. Her eyes frosted even more as she said to Lenny, "You're lucky I always hit what I'm aiming for."

"And you *were* going to kill me," Brock ground out. "A fact I'll be happy to testify to," he said as he pulled the man to the car. As mad as he was at the man, he wouldn't make him wait in the cold for the EMS. He wasn't giving Lenny anything else to complain about that would prolong their night.

"And I make a pretty good witness," Gisella offered. Then she sighed. "I'll meet you at the station. I guess I'm going to have a lot of paperwork to fill out tonight. Not to mention calling my captain and getting him to do some fancy talking so I'm not assigned a desk job while this is investigated."

Brock grimaced. "I'll have to wait on the EMS to get here. I'd transport him, but don't want to have to clean out my car. Speaking of which, there's a videotaped recording of everything that just happened. Your boss shouldn't have any trouble getting this cleared up ASAP."

A glimmer of respect finally reared its head. "That'll help a lot."

He nodded. "I'll get someone to take over for me and meet you in half an hour."

"I'll be waiting." She shot him a pointed look. "Again."

He gave her a slow smile and Gisella felt her heart tremble at his low, "I'll be there."

A little unnerved by the attraction she felt for a man she'd just met, she shook her head and headed for the vehicle she'd left parked on the other side of the trees.

Gisella had flown down from San Antonio, grabbed a cab and rushed to meet Brock Martin, one of the drug enforcement agents assigned to the El Paso area of the border.

El Paso was a twenty-minute drive from Boot Hill, which was a five-minute drive from Juarez, Mexico. Her objective was to pick Brock up and head straight to Boot Hill. She hadn't planned on getting sidetracked saving his life along the way.

But I guess You weren't ready for him to die yet, were You, Lord? Thanks for using me in this situation. Now, please, please help me find the ones responsible for the drug smuggling and the murder of Captain Pike.

For the past four months, Gisella and her company of Rangers had worked hard trying to gather the evidence needed to take down the organization responsible for their leader's murder. Just recently, she and her fellow Rangers had taken the information contained on the flash drive they'd found on Melora

Hudson's estate a few weeks ago and narrowed down the possibilities of where the drugs could be entering the country from across the border.

Melora's husband had been killed because of his association with the Lions of Texas, an elite group responsible for millions of dollars worth of drugs coming over the border, and Melora had almost been killed herself. Fortunately, they'd found what the killers were after and now the Lions had no reason to go after her anymore.

And thanks to the information on the flash drive, Boot Hill seemed to be the next logical choice in their hunt for the top members of the criminal organization. Gisella and the other Rangers believed the drugs coming into San Antonio, and all parts of Texas, were originating from that tiny, almost nonexistent blip on the map.

When Brock had failed to show up for their scheduled meeting a few hours earlier, she'd gotten tired of waiting around, did a little snooping and found out from one of the other agents where he was.

She'd punched in the location of the church in her GPS and driven straight there.

Not wanting to give herself away, she'd circled the building twice, then found a suitable parking spot that would enable her to be of some help should Brock need it, yet far enough away not to tip off the informant.

When she saw how Lenny had been acting, the hairs on her neck stood straight up. When that happened, she knew to pay attention. She'd pulled her weapon. Creeping in closer hadn't been a problem underneath the shelter of the trees.

Now, the ordeal was coming to a close. As she reached her vehicle, she heard the scream of sirens and saw the flashing lights of the approaching ambulance.

Help had arrived and she could get back to the office. Anxious to get on with her reason for being in El Paso, she drove with a single-minded purpose and thought about the man she would be working with.

A very good-looking—in a Brad Pitt sort of way—man. From the sandy blond hair and flashing blue eyes to the perfect smile. Her heart trembled at the memory of the smile that flashed white teeth and deep dimples. The fact that he probably hadn't shaved in two days didn't detract from his attractiveness at all. On the contrary, she liked the rugged look.

Gisella blinked at her thoughts. What in the world was she doing? She didn't think she even liked the man and she was daydreaming about how good-looking he was. When was the last time she'd done that?

She couldn't remember.

You're here for a reason, she reminded herself sternly. The mental admonishment brought her up short.

She was here to find a way to bring down the

Lions of Texas, a group responsible for the death of her boss, Captain Gregory Pike. The Lions had already made millions of dollars smuggling their drugs over the border from Mexico. Her desperate hope was that Brock Martin might have some answers for her on where their entry point was.

When she'd learned she was to be paired up with the drug enforcement agent, she'd done her homework and researched everything she could find on him.

Which wasn't much.

But she had learned that he'd been working the border for more than 10 years, was experienced and well-liked in his department. She hoped together they could pool their resources and bring down the Lions.

She parked at the entrance to EPIC—the El Paso Intelligence Center. Agencies currently represented in the building included the Drug Enforcement Agency and almost every division of law enforcement one could think of. Their job was to keep the border—and the citizens in the surrounding small towns and cities—safe.

And she was going to have a hand in that.

Climbing out of her car, she headed inside and made her way to the department she'd left only a couple of hours ago in order to rescue her temporary partner.

Sitting at her desk in the office she'd been assigned upon her arrival, she stared at the desk opposite hers.

Brock Martin. DEA agent. One who sometimes acted as the Lone Ranger. Sometimes followed the rules, sometimes not. But still, from all appearances, a good man who got the job done.

"Lord, I hope You'll let me in on this plan of Yours that seems to be unfolding."

"Talking to yourself?"

Gisella jerked at the deep voice and whirled to find Brock standing in the doorway looking at her. She felt the heat crawl into her neck and knew within seconds her cheeks would be fiery in spite of her olive skin. "Something like that. You got here fast."

He pulled off his gloves then shrugged out of his heavy coat to drape it over the back of his chair. As he lowered himself into the seat, he said, "Backup got there pretty quick. I didn't have to hang around much longer." He steepled his fingers under his chin. "So. We're going to be partners for a while, huh?"

"Looks that way." She tried to ignore how well he filled out his pullover gray sweatshirt and how his blue eyes regarded her with an intensity that seemed to reach into her very soul. She cleared her throat. "So...why didn't you have any backup tonight?"

"Not everybody takes backup with them when they meet an informant."

She eyed him. "The smart ones do."

He blinked. Then barked a laugh. "Right. Well, it just so happens that I had backup with me, but he got a call that his wife was in labor. Needless to say, I sent him on his way." He rubbed a hand across his lips then frowned. "I'll admit, Lenny surprised me. For over a year, the man has provided solid information—and made a small fortune off of me." He shrugged. "I had no reason to suspect tonight would be any different." Another pause as he looked at her. "I'm glad you tracked me down."

Without another word, she nodded. She was glad, too. His last sentence might be considered a thank you. She decided she liked him a little better after all.

"So, show me what you've got." He rolled his chair around so that he sat shoulder to shoulder with her. Unprepared for the sudden move or the next wave of awareness that shot through her, she gave a small jump. Wow, he smelled good—even after that tussle with Lenny.

She cleared her throat and reached into her briefcase. "All we have to go on right now is this information. It was on a flash drive that was found in Melora Hudson's house. She was married to a man who was involved in the Lions and was killed two years ago because of it. His body was only found recently—near a drug drop site. It just goes to show you that these people will stop at nothing to protect their interests." She waved the book at him. "I printed all of the information on the drive off and made this little black book here. I needed it on paper form to study. Anyway, so far, we've uncovered the fact that drug shipments are coming out of Juarez, Mexico."

"Which is why you're here, right?"

"Right. And here." She pointed to the initials B.H.TX. "This is Boot Hill, Texas. We've already figured that much out. However, the rest of this is gibberish to me. You, however, know the border, you know the towns, you know the people. Surely, if there's something in here, you'll be able to zero in on it."

He held out a hand and she placed the book in it. When she did, her knuckles brushed his palm and sent shivers dancing all the way up her arm.

Jerking back, she looked at him and saw the surprise and awareness on his face, too.

Before he could say anything, she blurted, "Look on page seven. There are a lot of initials and numbers we haven't been able to decipher. Like I said, we figured out Boot Hill, but the others…" She bit off her words. She was repeating herself and sounding like an idiot. Clearing her throat, she shrugged. "Would you take a look at those and see if anything comes to you?"

"Sure." His warm gaze lingered on her face a moment longer and she swallowed hard.

After what seemed like years, he let his blue eyes

fall to the book in front of him. "So," he drawled. "They sent you here all by yourself? With no back-up?"

"Excuse me?" She understood the question, she just hoped she misunderstood the meaning behind it.

"No offense, but this is a really sticky situation and…"

At his doubtful look, Gisella bristled. She hadn't misunderstood. And just when she was starting to think he wasn't all bad. "What? You don't think I can handle this assignment because I'm a woman?"

Disdain dripped from her voice but she didn't care. She had no use for men who thought because she was female and pretty, she was somehow less than capable. Did she need to remind him of who'd saved whom only a short time ago?

He must have read her thoughts because he backpedaled and held up a hand as though in surrender. "No, no. That's not what I'm saying—exactly. I'm just saying that this is an extremely dangerous playground. If these people find out about you and you were to get caught…" He swallowed. "I don't have to tell you what the consequences would be. I just have a hard time believing your superiors would choose someone…"

She turned her head so that she came nose to nose with him.

And lip to lip.

Putting some distance between them, she held on to her ire and said, "I'm a big girl, Martin. I can handle it. They *chose* me *because* I can handle it. So don't give me any grief about being a woman in a man's world. I won't listen to it." She refused to bring up the incident with the informant. If she hadn't proved herself there, it would be hopeless to get into a discussion with the man about her skills.

Over the years, she'd found arguing with the men in law enforcement about her abilities was fruitless. She just had to do her job, do it well and keep her mouth shut. She'd also found the old adage that actions spoke louder than words was true.

But Gisella's gut tightened at the thought of the added tension Brock's skepticism would bring to the table. She forced herself not to worry about it now. She'd just deal with it.

Like she had when she first became a Ranger and the men had looked at her with a mixture of disbelief that she'd infiltrated their ranks, and a haughty, arrogant assurance that she wouldn't be around long.

She'd proven them all wrong and was now a respected and well-thought-of member of Company D. But it definitely hadn't been an easy road to travel.

And while she might keep her cool and ignore a lot of stuff she considered silly, that didn't mean she didn't have a backbone. "Can we focus on what we need to do? You go over that book while I fill out these papers on the shooting."

He just looked at her for a moment. Then sighed. "Yeah, sure." He glanced down, then back up. "I didn't mean to offend you, I was just...concerned."

"No need to be," she clipped.

She'd already called Ben and filled him in on the shooting incident. He wasn't happy at the tap dancing he was going to have to do in order for her to continue her current investigation. After a shooting, an officer was generally placed on administrative leave during the investigation. But Ben had pull in a lot of places. And the videotape from Brock's car that she'd sent him would go a long way with Internal Affairs.

And he needed Gisella in Boot Hill, Texas, investigating.

After she finished the paperwork, Brock and Gisella spent the next hour and a half bouncing ideas off each other until Brock finally said, "I don't know. This could go on forever. I say we head to Boot Hill and start asking questions. We can see what turns up."

"That was my original destination until I was told we were going to be working together." A thought hit Gisella and she gave a startled laugh.

Brock blinked. "What's so funny?"

"I just realized that they didn't exactly send me down here all alone."

His right brow lifted. "No?"

"Guess that's why they paired us up. So you can

protect me." She batted her lashes and put on her most helpless expression.

A short laugh escaped him. He snorted, "Well, when you put it that way…" Brock glanced at his watch. "Get that look off your face. If we leave now, we can be there in twenty minutes."

Gisella turned serious and sucked in a thoughtful breath. "Yeah, let's do that. I'm going to check in with my boss again and give him an update."

He stood as she grabbed her phone, excitement lighting his weary eyes. "Then let's hit the road."

"Do you have a car? I took a cab from the airport, then borrowed one of the station's cars to come find you."

His lips twisted. "Sure, we can use mine. Or rather, the department's."

She wondered at the odd look on his face but didn't ask.

Instead, she looked at the clock. 8:07. She was starving. Her suitcase sat at her feet. "Fine, as long as you promise we'll get something to eat soon."

TWO

After a quick stop by Brock's apartment to throw some things into a small suitcase, the drive to Boot Hill, Texas, took approximately twenty minutes. Upon entering the small town with the sign proudly proclaiming their population to be 1,406, Brock eyed the woman sitting next to him.

She'd been on the phone most of the ride with a fellow Ranger. Levi someone. "How's our guy in the hospital?" she asked. "Has he come out of the coma yet?"

Coma? Guy in the hospital? Brock shot her a brief glance which she ignored. Seems like she'd neglected to fill him in on a few details.

"Right," she said. "Keep me in the loop, okay?"

She must have gotten an affirmative response because she said thanks and hung up. To Brock she said, "Sorry, that was my new captain, Ben Fritz."

"Who's in the hospital in a coma?" Brock asked.

"We're not sure who he is." Gisella reached down into the backpack she'd brought with her and pulled out a water bottle. She held it out to him and he refused. After she took a sip, she said, "We just know that he's somehow involved with the Lions of Texas and his name is Quin Morton. We haven't figured out his connection to the Lions yet, but we will. He was there when Captain Pike was murdered in his own home. Before Captain Pike died, we—the Ranger company—had gotten a text that Pike had something major to share with us. We were all to gather at his house so he could fill us in, but when we got there…" She paused and he glanced at her as he pulled into a parking spot in front of The Great Plate, the restaurant he'd heard had good home cooking.

"Yeah?" he prompted.

She cleared her throat. "When we got there, we found our captain dead and another man severely wounded. That man's been in a coma ever since and we've had no luck tracking down who he is. We're desperate for him to wake up and tell us who shot him and the captain. But so far, no luck." She grimaced. "And to top that off, someone tried to kill him just a few weeks or so ago so he's under 24/7 guard right now."

"Ouch."

She opened her door and climbed out. He saw her pull the edges of her heavy down coat tighter against her throat. He shivered in his own jacket as they moved toward the warmth of the restaurant.

"And this is what you've been working on for the past several months?"

"That's it. We're making progress, finding clues here and there, but we just can't seem to grab on to that final piece of information that will allow us to put it all together and capture the top guys."

"Yeah," he muttered. "I know how you feel. I've been working the border down here for years, catching the small fish. I just can't seem to get the information I need to catch the big dogs."

"And then we've got the Alamo celebration coming up in March. Our company is part of the security detail and we believe someone is targeting that celebration for some reason." She pulled the door open. "Hopefully the answer to that is somewhere in the info on the flash drive."

As Gisella stepped inside, she breathed in the scents of veggies and coffee. And was that a roast she smelled? Her stomach growled. A sudden longing for her mother's home cooking swept over her. *Please, Lord, let us resolve our differences soon.*

Brock stood behind her and for some reason, she was very aware of his presence. So much so that for a few seconds she didn't realize the noise level in the restaurant had dropped to a dead silence.

Although there weren't many customers—probably due to the lateness of the hour—all eyes present were focused on the newcomers. Gisella shifted, uncomfortable with the sudden attention. She was used to people staring out of curiosity simply because of her uniform and the fascination people had with Texas Rangers.

However, these stares didn't feel like that. They felt menacing. Surprised at her somewhat paranoid reaction, she let her eyes roam the restaurant again.

Nope, not paranoid. Unsmiling, stony faces looked back at her.

Then a man in a food-stained apron approached and handed them two menus. "Hey, I'm Angelo Luc—or Pop. I answer to both. Have a seat wherever you want, Krista'll be around shortly to take yer order. You got here just in time. I'm closing up in thirty minutes."

"Thanks." Gisella gripped her menu and made her way over to a booth in the corner. Brock slid in across from her and gradually, the patrons turned their attention back to their meals.

She blew out a breath. "What was that all about?"

"Small town, new faces?" He gestured toward her badge. "A Ranger in town and they want to know why."

Gisella flushed. "Maybe I should have changed and been a little less conspicuous. Then again, I'm not undercover and have nothing to hide."

"After we eat, I suggest we find the sheriff and explain our presence. I've already met him a few times but he'll want to know about you."

"Sounds good to me."

Brock picked up the menu. "So, what do you think? Lots of choices here."

She lifted a brow. "All five of them? That qualifies as a lot to choose from?"

A grin slid across his lips and she felt her face flush for a different reason this time. He was teasing her. Then his eyes flickered as he glanced at his options on the menu. "Choices. I've made a lot of choices in life."

"What kind of choices?"

"Right ones, wrong ones." He smirked. "Seems like the wrong ones outweigh the right ones some days."

Gisella blinked at his sudden flash of vulnerability. Where had that come from? But she knew what he meant. And because of that, she felt herself drawn to him. "I guess you have to pray about it and believe that God won't steer you wrong."

He pulled in a deep breath and studied her, his blue eyes piercing to her soul. "I haven't prayed in a long time."

More vulnerability. "Why not?" She couldn't help it, she was curious about him.

He flushed as though he regretted bringing up the topic, then shrugged. "I guess I've just been so busy trying to catch the bad guys, I haven't given God and prayer a lot of thought."

"That's understandable. I've been there."

"But you're not now?"

"No. God got my attention a few years ago. I finally realized I had to make the time to spend with Him, it wasn't just going to magically happen." She smiled, but didn't elaborate further.

She'd been mad at God for a long time after the death of her brother, but had eventually made her peace with it. A story she would be happy to share with the man before her. Maybe when she knew him a little better, though. She couldn't talk about it without tearing up. And after his doubtful comments about her superiors sending a woman down to work on this case, crying in front of Brock wasn't going to happen.

Brock kept silent, then seemed to realize she wasn't going to say anything else. He sighed. "Today when Lenny had that gun pointed at me and murder in his eyes…well, I have to say, I prayed."

"Guess God still has work for you to do."

"I guess." His smile finally touched his eyes.

"Whew! Sorry it took me so long to get over here. Y'all ready?"

They looked up to find a young girl probably not much older than sixteen standing at the edge of the table, pen poised above her order tablet. Her blond ponytail swung behind her and her blue eyes smiled with her lips.

Brock smiled back at her. "I'll take the special."

Gisella shut her menu. "Make that two."

"Country fried chicken, gravy, greens and corn-bread. You got it." She spun on her heel and headed for the kitchen.

Gisella let her eyes wander around the restaurant. Another young waitress worked the back tables. "Nice little place they have here. How did you find it?"

"A drug runner I arrested about a month ago was from here. He jumped bail and I was determined to get him back. I teamed up with a bounty hunter and we tracked him down. Found him holed up in his mother's attic about two miles from here."

"Probably part of the organization we're trying to eliminate."

"Now that wouldn't surprise me."

"So that's when you met the sheriff?"

"One of the times. I come through here occasionally on business."

The waitress came back and placed their drinks and a couple of straws on the table. Gisella took a sip of her water and leaned back. "You're not a very by-the-book kind of guy, are you?"

"What makes you ask that?" he deadpanned.

She gave a short laugh. "Right."

The food appeared on the table with a flourish and Krista asked them if they needed anything else. Gisella smiled at her. "No, this looks great, thanks."

"Just holler if you need something then."

"How old are you?" Gisella asked the girl.

"Sixteen."

So, she'd guessed right. "You're very good at this waitressing thing."

The girl gave a giggle. "Thanks. I don't normally work school nights, but two of the regular waitresses are out sick with the flu so…" She shrugged. "I told Pop—my grandfather—I'd help him."

"Very kind of you."

"Yeah, well, I'm not totally selfless. I like the money. Enjoy." She flashed another smile and twirled back to the kitchen.

"At least she's friendly," Brock said after a bite of his chicken.

Gisella didn't bother to answer as she tucked into her food.

The next ten minutes passed in relative silence as they both ate and tried not to let the stares from the remaining few customers faze them.

Gisella finally put down her fork and leaned back. "I'm stuffed. Reminds me of Mom's cooking." Cooking that she hadn't had a lot of lately. But that was her fault.

"Where are you from?" Brock lifted his glass and took another drink.

"San Antonio. Well, my parents are from Mexico originally, but I was born in Texas."

He smiled his thanks as Krista refilled their

glasses then turned his focus on Gisella. "Did you bring that little black book in?"

"Yes." She tilted her head and eyed him. "It's in my bag."

"I want to have another look at some of the other letters and numbers again."

"Sure." She reached into her purse and pulled out the book.

He took it, opened it and read aloud. "JZ, RP, QV. And the mixture of numbers and letters: 3149NJZ-10724WRPQV. JZ, RP and QV could all be initials, maybe? As for the other symbols, it could be a safe combination written in code. Or the numbers could be someone's birthday. 3149. Could that be March 1, 1949?"

"Possibly."

"And 10724."

"October 7th, 1924."

"And look, the letters JZ are repeated in the string of letters and numbers as well as RP and QV." Brock gave a frustrated grunt. "Could be anything."

He turned the page. "Look at this list of numbers."

"I know. I'm wondering if those are actually the dates and the numbers on the other page are something else."

She studied the list.

Brock shook his head. "Doesn't look like dates to me although I guess they could be." He rubbed his chin. "This shouldn't be that complicated. I think we're making it harder than it is." At her expression, he held up a hand. "I'm not saying all drug runners are stupid, but it looks like it made the rounds, passed from one member to the next. Surely they'd have to have some kind of common code or something so that whoever had the book could easily decipher it."

Gisella tapped a finger against her lips. "Agreed, but it would have to be complicated enough so that if it fell into the wrong hands," she wiggled her fingers at him, "such as yours truly, they wouldn't have to worry about it being decoded."

He grunted. "Okay. True."

"And look at this." She reached over, her fingers brushing his as she flipped the pages until she reached the back of the small book. Ignoring the wave of butterflies that took flight in her stomach when she touched him, she pointed. "Here are some symbols. This one takes up the whole page."

"Weird."

"I'm wondering if it's some kind of land form. Could be a lake, but we had our forensics person run it through the computer database to see if it matched up with anything around this area. It didn't."

He flipped the page. "What's this?" He referred to a series of lines that crisscrossed each other.

"Beats me." She shrugged and sighed. "Another symbol we don't have a clue about. We thought it might be a map of some roads. See the Y here? And here it almost looks like a U-turn that leads back to the main road leading from…well, from wherever it started. Our forensic people actually came up with a few possibilities, but when we checked them out, they were dead ends."

His expression stilled and he closed the book in a casual move. "We have company." His low voice snapped her from her calculated musings about the numbers, letters and symbols.

Glancing toward the door she saw three men in uniforms headed their way. Pulling her drink toward her, she relaxed and pasted a friendly smile on her face.

The three men took the table next to Gisella's and Brock's booth and the man who was obviously the sheriff leaned back in his chair and adjusted his hat. He placed his right ankle on his left knee and nodded in their direction. "Howdy, folks."

"Hello," Gisella answered. "Sheriff?"

"I am. Sheriff Kip Johnston." He pointed to the man on his left. "Meet Niles Vernon, a Border Patrol agent working out of the Boot Hill border crossing station, and Chris Locke, one of my deputies."

Gisella offered him a smile. "I'm Ranger Gisella Hernandez," she said, "and this is Agent Brock Martin with the DEA. I think you two have met before. We were just saying we needed to come over to your office and let me introduce myself."

Brock nodded his greeting and held out his hand. "Good to see you again, Sheriff."

The sheriff and Brock shook hands. "Yep, I remember you. It's been a while, hasn't it?"

"I haven't had any more escapees who headed this way."

Sheriff Johnston gave a small laugh.

Krista came by and took the men's order then disappeared again.

Chris Locke settled into his chair then shot them a narrow-eyed look. "So let's get right to it. What are you in town for? I mean Boot Hill's so small you'd miss it if you blinked. What brings a Ranger and a DEA agent to our fair town?"

Gisella decided she wasn't so sure she liked this deputy and focused her attention on the friendlier Niles Vernon and Sheriff Johnston. "We're here investigating a possible connection with the Lions of Texas. Have you heard of them?"

The sheriff took a swig of his drink before saying, "Nope. Who are they?"

"We believe they're responsible for a lot of things, the main one being the death of a fellow Ranger. We think our friend found out something about the Lions and they killed him."

The sheriff winced. "Sorry to hear that."

Gisella swallowed hard. She always got emotional when she thought about Captain Gregory Pike. She pushed her sadness away and said, "Anyway, we also believe they're running drugs big time. These drugs are finding their way throughout the state of Texas and Boot Hill is a possible entry point from Mexico for them."

Chris snorted. "Boot Hill's not perfect and not crime-free, but we keep the drugs out. If they make it over the border, they get stopped here." He shook his head. "The drugs spreading through Texas aren't coming through Boot Hill."

Instead of commenting, Gisella simply nodded. "What about you, Sheriff? Do you have any reason to believe these people are working out of Boot Hill?"

Before the sheriff could respond, Niles interrupted with an irritated look at Chris. "Regardless of what my buddy here thinks, it's possible some drugs do get into Boot Hill. But Chris's right about one thing, it would be mighty hard. We've got the Border Patrol station and we police the fence closely with agents and K-9s."

The sheriff didn't lose his scowl. He did raise a thoughtful brow. "In spite of Chris's protests, we all know that in spite of our best efforts, the drugs slip through."

"I will say that if it's coming across—and I'm not saying it's not—it's coming across on somebody else's watch," Niles grunted.

"Not on mine." Chris rolled his eyes, shrugged then gave a sneer. "And we don't need some fancy-pants Ranger or DEA agent coming in and stirring up trouble."

"Cool it, Locke," Sheriff Johnston ordered softly.

Chris rolled his eyes, sat back and gave his recently delivered food his full attention.

Niles shot them an apologetic look.

Gisella wondered what the deputy's problem was then decided to ignore it. "So, Sheriff, what do you say we team up and work together? I think if we're sharing information and backing each other up, we'll be able to find what we're looking for a lot faster."

"Work together, huh?"

"Well, we're either working together or we're not. To me the choice is a simple one."

Sheriff Johnston stroked his chin while Chris Locke looked on. "This town isn't so friendly to outsiders."

Gisella felt one side of her mouth lift in a smile. "We noticed. Hopefully, if they see us cooperating with each other, they'll warm up to us."

Niles grunted and Chris ignored them.

Brock said, "We need a couple of hotel rooms. Got any suggestions?"

The sheriff smiled. "If you want to stay in Boot Hill, your only option is the Boot Hill Inn. You can walk to it from here if you don't mind a little hike. They have twenty-two rooms total."

"Any vacancies?"

"Guess you'll have to go find out. But yeah,

probably. We don't get a lot of visitors except families needing a place to stay during the holidays. The Christmas rush is over so you'll probably have your pick of the rooms." He leaned forward and wiped his mouth with his napkin. "So how long do you figure you're going to be staying here?"

Gisella firmed her jaw and looked the sheriff in the eye. "As long as it takes."

THREE

In the hotel office, Brock studied the man behind the counter and wondered vaguely what his story was. He'd been wiping down the counter with a rag when they'd walked in. His nametag read, STEVE.

A white scar cut a path from his forehead, down his right cheek to his chin. Prison tats decorated his fingers and his eyes had a hard glint to them. Gisella's tense shoulders said she had her guard up, too.

Brock didn't like the fact that Steve's eyes had lingered a little long on Gisella's pretty face, but Brock had to give the man credit. He hadn't looked at her in any way that could be considered disrespectful. He simply handed over her credit card and room key and said, "Thank you. Glad you're here."

Gisella gave him a friendly nod.

Steve said, "There's two of us who run the front desk. We alternate shifts and cover for each other so you never know who'll be up front. We only have one maid working right now. We're not a big-city hotel, so if you need something I'll do my best to get it to you, but don't expect to get it right away." He spoke in a flat monotone as though he didn't want them there, but couldn't afford to turn them away.

Brock nodded. "We'll keep that in mind."

Gisella said to Brock, "I'm going to step outside and make a phone call while you're finishing up."

"I'll be there in a minute."

While he repeated the process Gisella had just completed, Brock considered the twinge of jealousy he'd felt at the hotel clerk's obvious admiration of Gisella and told himself to get real.

He'd only known the woman a few hours. How could he be jealous? That he was made him a little nervous. Brock signed the credit card slip and thanked the man. Steve nodded and returned to his cleaning without another word.

Brock stepped outside to find Gisella already sitting in the passenger seat with her door shut. He decided he liked seeing her there. Beside him, she tugged at the heart with occasional glimpses of her vulnerability. He admired her tough-as-nails attitude about her job.

Climbing into the driver's seat, he looked at her. "Too cold to stand outside for very long, huh?"

She laughed and agreed.

"You get your call made?"

Gisella frowned. "He didn't answer."

"Who?"

"My dad."

"And that worries you?"

She shrugged. "No. He and my mom are probably out with their friends from church. He's left a couple messages on my phone so I thought I'd try him back. No big deal." She gave him a wry smile. "Trust me, he'll call again."

Brock drove about halfway down the building and parked in the almost empty lot, not in front of a room. "Our rooms are four doors up."

Respect gleamed at him. "I never park in front of my door, either. Why advertise what room you're in?"

He laughed. "Exactly. I try to make sure I don't park in front of anyone else's room either. Wouldn't want an innocent person to get hurt because someone was looking for me."

"You think someone's going to come looking for us?"

He shrugged. "I don't know. This town isn't exactly Mayberry. The sheriff and our rough-looking desk clerk didn't seem thrilled that we're here and from what you've told me, a lot of people have died because of this case. If anyone here has connections with the Lions, then they're aware we're here and that we're asking questions. Why take chances?"

"I agree." She smiled and climbed from the car.

Brock watched Gisella haul her overnight bag from the car. "You need some help?"

She shot him a wry look. "I think I can handle it, thanks."

Inserting the key into the lock, she slipped into her room.

Brock shook his head. Stubborn. And very pretty. What was her boss thinking, sending her into this situation? In spite of the fact that Gisella was confident in her abilities to take care of herself, Brock's gut clenched as he thought about his former partner, Paul Gomez, and his experience. Paul had had a pretty female partner, too, once upon a time. Tina Lorenzo. Paul had fallen in love with her and she'd been killed.

Brock had been paired up with the man after the tragedy. Paul had lasted three months before quitting law enforcement altogether to see if he could find himself at the bottom of a bottle.

Poor Paul. He'd been planning on asking Tina to marry him the weekend that she was killed. Had even bought the ring and shown it around the station that day. Tina had been working an undercover assignment, one she and Paul had argued about. He hadn't wanted her to take it. She'd insisted.

Brock blew out a sigh. Was he going to have to babysit the Ranger?

Maybe not if her saving his hide tonight hadn't been a fluke. He still wasn't sure how Lenny had gotten the drop on him. But he had. And Brock felt embarrassed that Gisella had witnessed it.

On the other hand, it gave him an idea of who she was. And Brock wasn't against females in law enforcement. Not at all. He knew there were some good women cops. Had even worked with a few. But this whole situation was a different ballgame as far as he was concerned. The Lions had all kinds of connections. High-ranking ones, apparently. They didn't hesitate to permanently remove anyone who got in their way. And mistakes were always fatal. What if Giselle's bulldog determination to catch her boss's killer caused her to be careless? Make a mistake? She could get them both killed.

And the powers that be in the Ranger department had sent a lone woman down here to investigate. What were they thinking?

Of course he was with her, but still…

Just as he was about to step back inside his own hotel room, Gisella appeared in the doorway next to his. "You all set?" he asked.

She looked up to meet his eyes and his blood pumped a little faster. She had beautiful big brown eyes. Eyes that made a man want to act like a brainless sap and get lost in them. He blinked.

"You bet." She gave him a funny smile. "You?"

He nodded then said, "But sleep with your gun close by. These locks are pitiful."

She bent to examine hers. "Actually, it's not that bad."

He grunted his disagreement. Gisella shook her

head in amusement then said with understanding, "But I know what you mean. My locks at home are much better." She gave him another soft smile that made his heart do things it hadn't done in a long time. He gulped and ordered himself not to be attracted to her.

It didn't work.

And that sent fear skittering through him. Memories of his fiancée's betrayal flashed across his mind, but this time they didn't seem to hold as much punch.

And it was easy to see Gisella wasn't anything like the woman who'd left him for another man. A man with a safe job who would be home every night and wouldn't be gone for months at a time. He'd done his best to keep in touch, doing small things to remind her that he was thinking of her—like having the florist deliver a rose to her once a week.

But it hadn't been enough and she'd moved on.

He nearly smiled at the irony of it. Gisella would understand his job, what going undercover entailed. And she understood that because she lived it.

And yet, Brock refused to consider falling for someone he worked with, someone in as dangerous a profession as he was. Thinking about the possible results of loving someone who could be killed in the blink of an eye made him shudder. He simply knew too much about things that could go wrong, how easy it was to slip up, trust the wrong person.

Ignoring his thumping heart that didn't seem to care what Gisella did for a living, he tuned back into her words. "In the morning we can start out by asking around about those other initials from the book. See if there's anyone around here with the initials JZ, RP or QV."

"Sounds good to me. See you in the morning." He stepped into his room and shut the door.

Slowly, Gisella closed her door, absently thinking that someone needed to oil the squeaky hinges— then decided she was thankful for the built-in alarm system. She leaned against the metal door for a moment, pausing to stare at the ceiling.

Breathing out a sigh, she placed a hand over her pounding heart. "What in the world is going on, Lord? He's just an attractive man. I work around a lot of attractive men and I don't even notice them much other than to give them credit for doing a good job. What's different about Brock Martin?"

Not getting an immediate answer, she finally took in the details of the room. It smelled clean. Simple and sparse and not much to it; nevertheless, the bed looked comfortable.

Part of her itched to take a dive into a pool and do several laps to work off the stress of the day. Something she did at home on a regular basis.

Not holding out much hope, she walked to the phone and dialed the front desk. When the man answered, she asked, "You wouldn't happen to have an indoor pool, would you?"

"Yes, we do. Right here beside the office." He told her how to get to it and she hung up, surprise zipping through her. Who would have thought?

She placed her laptop on the small round table by the window and turned it on.

Weariness tugged at her and she glanced at the clock. 11:46. Morning would come early. But work beckoned. So did the swim.

Choices.

She thought about Brock's comment about choices in life and smiled. Sometimes you chose what you *had* to do, not what you *wanted* to do.

The swim would have to wait.

Gisella picked up her cell phone and punched in Levi McDonnell's number.

He answered on the third ring. "McDonnell."

"Hey, it's Gisella."

"Yeah, I recognized the number. What's up?"

"Sorry to call so late. I wanted to ask for a quick update."

"It's been kind of quiet. There haven't been any new threats against the Alamo celebration coming up, but we don't know if that's good or bad. Have they stopped sending threats because they realize they've made their point? Or have the threats stopped because of something else? We just don't know."

She blew out a sigh. "Right. Anything else?"

"Nope." His voice softened. "Get some rest, Gisella, you're going to need it. We're getting closer to getting these people, I can feel it."

"I sure hope so, Levi."

"Talk to you soon."

They hung up and Gisella decided Levi was right; she needed to get some rest.

But first, she was going to get her swim in.

Grabbing her towel and the one-piece black bathing suit she never left home without, she slipped into her heavy coat, hat and gloves.

Should she tell Brock what she was doing?

Maybe.

Then again, he already had his doubts about her ability to be here on this case by herself. If he thought she felt the need to report in to him to take a swim, he really would think she was in over her head.

Gisella scoffed. She'd been doing just fine all alone. She didn't need him as a keeper. She ignored the small voice that said perhaps it was just common courtesy to let him know where she was going and assured herself that she was only going to be a few minutes. Besides, it was late. She didn't want to wake him if he was sleeping.

She was quite confident in her ability to take care of herself—and she didn't plan on staying long.

Opening the door, she made her way down the

sidewalk and headed toward the office, keeping an eye out for the pool sign.

As she walked, out of habit, she scanned the area, taking full advantage of the meager lighting the hotel offered. With surprise she noted how neat everything was. The trimmed bushes, the overpowering smell of freshly-spread mulch. She paused. Who laid mulch in January?

Interesting.

The silence tickled her ears.

Nothing moved in the darkness.

A room door clicked shut somewhere behind her and she turned to look over her shoulder.

Nothing.

Her stomach twisted as she took in the quiet night. At home, she tended to enjoy the darkness, the quiet peacefulness that came with the setting sun.

Here, she felt exposed in the openness, wishing she had some kind of cover to hide behind. Hugging the building, she hurried along. She wondered if she should have brought her weapon with her. But she'd left it in the room, not wanting to leave it lying out of reach while she was in the pool.

Now, she was thinking that leaving it behind might not have been a good idea.

Sudden laughter spilled from the balcony above and she felt her muscles relax. Slightly. The two college guys had the door to their room open allowing bits and pieces of conversation to drift down to her.

Absently, she thought they must be crazy to have the door open on a cold night like tonight, but to each his own, she supposed.

The feeling of being watched lingered and she shivered. Looking around netted her nothing new.

Taking the sidewalk in front of the office building, she saw the sign indicating the pool facility. A concrete structure, it had small horizontal windows running along the length at the very top. The double glass doors that led to the interior were tinted and— she tried one—unlocked.

Slipping inside, she saw she was the only one there. She supposed those who had come to swim had done so earlier in the day.

There weren't that many people in the small hotel. She and Brock had done their homework on the ride over from the restaurant. The other occupants consisted of a family of three who had one room at the end of the building, an elderly couple in the room above hers and a couple of college kids passing through Boot Hill on their way to a family funeral. And that was it. Which suited her just fine.

Gisella found the changing room. Chlorine assaulted her nose and a tingle of anticipation crept up her spine. At home, she had an inground heated pool that she used at every opportunity.

If she was home, that was daily. If she was on a case, she found the nearest pool to work off the stress. If she couldn't swim, she'd go for a run, but she preferred the peaceful feel of the water.

With one foot, she tested the temperature.

Perfect. Who would have thought this small-town hotel would have an adequate pool like this?

Gisella walked to the deep end and looked down. More meager lighting, she thought ruefully. There were underwater lights, but they didn't do much more than offer a faint glow. She didn't care. With a push of her feet, she plunged into the warm depths.

With each stroke she felt the stress of the day slide from her. Her strong arms ate up the distance and soon she flipped and pushed off from the other end.

Brock Martin. DEA. A bit on the rough side. A risk-taker.

A good-looking man that made her heart do things it hadn't done in a really long time. Not since Andre. A mistake she'd promised herself she wouldn't repeat. He'd been a hard worker, a fellow Highway Patrol.

And he'd hated that her goal was to become a Ranger. He'd felt threatened by her skills and her determination to achieve her goals. So, he'd left her. But not before Gisella had learned a lesson. Steer clear of men whose egos couldn't handle a woman in her position. And don't be sucked in by a pretty face.

Brock definitely fell into the pretty-face category.

But was there more to him than his looks?

She had a feeling she would be finding that out during the course of the investigation.

Lord, keep us safe. Help us find Greg's murderer and stop more innocent people from dying.

As she swam, she prayed. A habit she'd started in her teen years before her brother, José, had died. After his death, she'd been mad at God for a long time, but found swimming and praying helped. Soon, she'd made her peace with God, but not with the drugs that killed José.

His death had made her what she was today.

Finally, she tired and decided to call it quits.

Just as she reached the side to pull herself out, she felt something encircle her wrist.

FOUR

Adrenaline spiking, she twisted her wrist, grasped the hand that held her and yanked. She was rewarded with a resounding splash behind her. Sputtering, her feet touching bottom, she whirled to see Brock treading water, his jaw tight, his face grim.

"What in the world is wrong with you?" she gasped.

"You could let a partner know where you're going."

Gisella stared at him, words failing her. She narrowed her eyes. "I don't report to you."

His jaw didn't soften, but she thought his eyes did. A fraction. "No, you don't. And I shouldn't have grabbed you like that. I called your name twice, you were so lost in your water world, you didn't hear me." He moved to the shallow end and got his footing.

Shock zipped up her spine. Swallowing hard, Gisella wilted against the side of the pool. "Really?"

"Yeah. That's not safe. You need to be more aware."

Her pride stung. He was right. When she swam, she tuned everything out. At home, she had her security system. Here, it was just her and Brock against the town of Boot Hill. At least that was what it felt like.

Gisella hauled herself out of the pool. Brock followed her. He tossed her a towel and she buried her face in it, buying time. But there was only one thing she could say. "You're right."

Her soft answer wiped out his anger. "Oh. Okay then. Good." Clearing his throat, he admitted with a rueful smile, "I have to admit, you have great reflexes and reaction skills."

Gisella gave a small laugh and shook her head. "At home, I swim all the time. I don't think about work or the danger or..." She pulled in a breath. "I was wrong. I don't have that option here. I should have told you what I was doing." She changed the subject. "What made you come looking for me?"

"I heard someone at my door. I thought it might be you."

She frowned. "Someone with the wrong room?"

He shrugged. "Maybe. Thinking it was you, I called out that I was coming. By the time I looked out the window, whoever was there was gone. I went back inside and called your room. When you didn't answer, I got a little concerned."

"So you checked the pool?"

"It seemed logical. You said you liked to swim off stress and the hotel has a pool."

Gisella felt her insides warm. He was worried about her. Part of her appreciated it. The other was embarrassed that he'd called her out on her carelessness. But she considered herself a big girl. She could handle it. "You need to get your gun dried out."

He quirked a smile as he looked down at his sopping clothes. "Along with everything else."

Standing, she wrapped the towel around her. "Let me change into dry clothes. Once I get back to my room, I promise to stay there, all right?"

He smiled. "Sure."

She gave him a head-to-toe glance. "You're going to freeze on the walk back."

Brock shrugged. "I'll live."

A few minutes later she'd changed back into her clothes, pulled her hair up and wrapped the towel around it. On the trek back to her room, she noticed the stillness that hung heavy in the dark air.

She shivered. Not just from the cold, but from the feeling that eyes watched her progress. Again.

Brock walked silently beside her, tension emanating from him along with the occasional shiver. He hunched his shoulders and picked up the pace.

"You feel it here, too, don't you?" she asked.

"It's too quiet," he agreed in almost a whisper. "Crickets should be chirping. There should be some kind of night sounds."

"But there's not. It's totally creepy." She paused in front of her door. "Thanks."

"For?" He lifted a brow in amusement.

She huffed. "You know what for."

Brock smiled and gave a small bow—followed by a racking shudder. "My pleasure."

Without thinking, she reached up and touched his mouth with a forefinger. "Your lips are blue."

His eyes narrowed. "I can think of a great way to warm them."

Gisella breathed a laugh. "I bet you can. Good night, Brock."

Within seconds, she let herself into her room. "Whew." She liked him. A lot.

But she really didn't need to flirt with him. Not when he had doubts about her.

Powering down the computer she hadn't touched, she felt anger begin to burn. Anger with herself.

She'd been careless, thoughtless.

Even though there'd been no direct threats made against her or Brock, she'd ignored her instincts and pushed aside her internal warnings. She could have put herself in danger.

Vowing not to make that mistake again, she walked to the window and gently pushed aside the curtain to look out.

Brock's car sat four doors down, right where he'd left it.

Nothing moved outside that she could see.

So what was her anxiety all about?

After checking the safety on her weapon, she slid it under her pillow. Exhaustion pounded on her and without bothering to dry her hair, she stretched out on the bed. More prayers drifted heavenward as she thought about her fellow Rangers back in San Antonio working the case from their end.

So much heartache had occurred because of the Lions—and yet the case had brought a lot of good people together, too, such as Ben and Corinna.

She flipped over and closed her eyes.

Would this case bring her and Brock together? Or in the end push them far apart?

Only time would tell.

The next thing she knew, she jerked awake, heart pounding. She'd fallen asleep fully clothed as she often did at home. Never a good sleeper, if she got sleepy on the couch, that's where she stayed.

Swinging her legs over the side of the bed, she sat there and listened. What had awakened her?

The sound of a car door slamming? Not so unusual. She was at a hotel. But no, that wasn't it.

Another sound. A loud whoosh.

Outside her door? No, but close.

Shrugging off the fog of sleep, she moved toward the window.

Pushing the curtain aside, she gasped at the flames spurting from Brock's vehicle.

FIVE

Brock jolted at the sound of the explosion and raced for the door. Yanking it open, he and several other onlookers, the few hotel guests and a homeowner from across the street, gaped.

His car spewed flames. The night clerk, Steve, stood with a phone in his hand shaking his head at the sight.

Sirens sounded in the distance and Brock turned to see Gisella standing in her doorway watching the burning vehicle through narrowed eyes. If her jaw got any tighter, it would shatter.

Walking over, he reached out to grip her bicep. She jerked and looked at him. Leaning over, he said in her ear, "Scan the crowd. Do you see anyone who looks satisfied? Like he's just done a good job?"

"Just the clerk," she muttered.

Brock had to admit, she was right. The clerk, still on the phone, listened to something his caller said and laughed, shooting a smirk in Brock's and

Gisella's direction. "This town sure doesn't seem to like outsiders, does it?"

Drawing in a deep breath, she planted her hands on her hips. "Apparently not." A small tight smile curved her lips, but didn't reach her eyes. "We've only been in town a couple of hours and we've already made someone nervous."

"Seriously nervous," Brock muttered, watching, scanning, looking for anyone who looked suspicious. Even though he'd parked four doors down, the heat reached him and he stepped back, pulling Gisella with him out of reach of the expanding fire.

"So, this is a warning," she said. A statement, not a question.

"Oh, yeah. They're letting us know they're not happy we're here." He shifted for a better angle of the corner of the building to his left. Was that simply a shadow? Nope, it moved. Shadows only moved when someone made them move.

From the corner of his eye, he caught her frown. She muttered, "I don't want to say they're all stupid, but blowing up our car sure isn't going to make me want to leave. In fact, it just makes me want to find who did this even more." The hard set to her jaw told him more than words. She had a stubborn streak as big as his.

Brock narrowed his eyes on the shape in the distance. It moved again. "Exactly. Looks like we're on the right track."

"So, you wanna stick around town a little longer?" she drawled as she crossed her arms in front of her.

Fire trucks pulled into the hotel parking lot and the firemen got busy.

"Like you told the sheriff, for as long as it takes." He frowned. "I'm surprised they have a fire department."

"Probably strictly volunteer," she muttered. "You know this isn't going to be the last *warning* we get."

"Nope. They know that we now know that they don't want us here. We're going to have to be extra careful until we figure out who's friend and who's foe."

"Whatever you're staring at—is he a friend or a foe?"

Brock cut his eyes to her. So, she'd already learned to read him pretty well. Nonplussed, he wasn't sure how he felt about that. "That's what I've been wondering. Want to go find out?"

"After you."

As inconspicuously as possible, Brock headed in the direction of the person he'd seen watching. A person who appeared to be attempting to melt into the shadows, not wanting to be noticed.

If that person were innocent, why hide in the shadows and watch? Why not come closer and join the rapidly expanding crowd?

Aware of Gisella right behind him, he unholstered his weapon. She slipped her hand into the crook of his arm and tossed him a charming smile causing his heart to two-step a happy dance. "Act like you're not watching him," she gritted through the smile.

He felt the flush creep up under his collar and was grateful for the darkness and poorly lit walkway. Her hand felt like it might burn a hole through his shirt. He leaned closer to act like he might say something to her while keeping his eyes on the spot where he saw the shadow. "You see him?" he whispered.

"Yes."

And so did Brock. The shadow moved once more, then running footsteps reached his ears.

Gisella released his arm like it singed her, and yelled, "Freeze! Texas Ranger!" To Brock, she said, "He's got a ski mask on and he's heading for the back alley."

She took off after the fleeing individual.

Brock bolted after her, rounding the corner of the building and ignoring the smell of rotting refuse. What if the man had a gun? A knife? More of whatever he used to set the car on fire?

Gut churning, he pumped his legs faster and rounded another corner to see Gisella leap over a heap of trash in one smooth move. A dim light at the back of the hotel illuminated the area enough that he could make out the man ahead of her.

Brock watched him slam into the eight-foot-high chain-link fence and climb it like he'd practiced doing it a few hundred times.

Gisella hit the fence to climb after the man, her movements not quite as smooth. Then she seemed to hit her stride, caught up, and got a hand on his ankle.

Brock waited at the foot of the fence fully expecting her to yank the man off balance. Instead, the fleeing suspect's foot shot out and caught Gisella in the side of her head. She gave a muffled yelp and released her grip to fall straight toward Brock.

For the brief moment she hung suspended in midair, Gisella wondered how bad the impact with the asphalt was going to hurt.

Then something caught her around the waist and she landed with a thud.

On something softer than the ground, but hard enough to knock the breath out of her.

Stunned, she simply lay there. As she was finally able to pull in a lung full of air, she became aware of a rhythmic thumping against her left ear.

Brock.

Gasping, she scrambled to the side.

He gave a wheezing cough and asked, "Are you all right?"

"Yes." She pulled in a steadying breath. "At least, I think so. Are you?"

He sat up and flexed his arms. "Looks like it." He eyed her. "For a skinny little thing, you sure are solid."

She narrowed her gaze on him. "You want the breath knocked out of you again?"

Holding up his hands in mock horror, he drew in another breath. "No, ma'am. Once a day is plenty for me."

Gisella got to her feet and glared at the fence in disgust. Only then did the pounding in her right temple register. She winced and pressed a hand to the area. No blood. That was good. "I'd call for help, but I figure that guy is long gone by now." She paused. "And I left my cell phone in the room."

She looked up to see Brock's concerned gaze on her, all teasing gone. "I left mine, too. Are you sure you're okay?" he asked.

She waved a hand. "I'm fine. Really. I got lucky. It was just a glancing blow. A couple of aspirin and I'll be good as new." She smiled. "Thanks for the cushion. If you hadn't caught me, I would really be hurting right now."

His lips quirked in a half smile. "After the debacle with my informant, I figured I owed you a soft landing."

She laughed. "Right."

"Come on. Let's go see what's going on. Surely someone in law enforcement is going to want a statement from us. Did you get a look at him?"

"No." She firmed her lips into a frustrated line.

"He had a ski mask on. I think his eyes are brown, though. The streetlight reflected on him for a second before he disappeared."

Brock gave a short laugh. "We're five miles from the border of Mexico. Almost everyone's eyes are brown."

Gisella shrugged. "True."

Together, they made their way back to the front of the hotel, watching the shadows and wondering who'd left them such a scorching present.

As they rounded the corner, Gisella spied the car across the parking lot. A smoking shell remained. Firefighters still stood on guard to make sure they'd gotten the fire completely out. "I'm glad we got most of our stuff out of your car before that happened."

Brock sighed and rubbed his eyes. "Yeah. My captain isn't going to like this one bit, though."

Gisella peered up at him through her lashes, the expression on his face making her wonder. "Hmm."

"What does that mean?"

She smirked and gestured to the car. "What number is that one?"

Innocence flared as his eyebrows shot skyward. "What makes you ask that?"

Gisella crossed her arms in front of her stomach. "Brock, how many department cars have you killed?"

The innocence disappeared and his cheeks turned red. "Aw, man, how did you…" His lip curled in disgust. "Counting that one? Three." He held up a hand. "But scout's honor, just like this one, the others were beyond my control, too."

She shook her head and looked to see Sheriff Johnston heading their way. The thunderous look on his face didn't bode well.

"Sheriff." Brock nodded at him. "Thanks for coming so fast. I apologize for the inconvenience."

"Inconvenience?" Incredulous, he stared at them. "Someone blew up your car in the middle of our hotel parking lot! I wouldn't call that an inconvenience. I'd call that... I'd call that...well..." He threw his hands in the air. "I don't rightly know what I'd call that." If the vein in the sheriff's temple pounded any harder, Gisella feared he might have a stroke.

She spoke. "Looks like someone doesn't like us being here, they've just made that more than obvious. I'm sorry, Sheriff. We're not here to cause you problems, we're here to try and solve some. And we really can't do that without your help."

Her soft words seemed to have the desired effect and his face lightened one shade of red, although his eyes stayed in squint mode. "I would say you're right about that, little lady."

Gisella grimaced at the moniker, but held her tongue. "Who knew we were staying here?"

Chris Locke arrived in time to hear her question and gave a humorless laugh. "Just about everyone in town five minutes before you left the diner."

"Or anyone who drove past the hotel and spotted the car that shouts 'cop,'" the sheriff added. "We're a border town. Not everyone who lives here has a fondness for law enforcement. This could have nothing to do with you two personally, it could just be someone's sick way of saying, 'We don't like cops.'"

Brock sighed and Gisella felt a mind-numbing weariness chase away the adrenaline rush she'd been going on for the past thirty minutes. She didn't think it was someone who just saw their car and decided to burn it because it belonged to a couple of cops. This definitely felt personal.

Like a message. A warning.

But the sheriff was entitled to his opinion.

"All right, we need to look at any footage from the security cameras." She paused. "There are security cameras, right?"

Brock rubbed his cheek. "One way to find out. Let's find the hotel clerk and ask."

The sheriff shook his head. "I'm going to finish taking statements and see if there are any witnesses."

Together, Gisella and Brock walked into the office to question the desk clerk. For the first time, Gisella really took note of the office. It was actually quite nice. The plaid furniture looked fairly new and the flat-screen television in the corner was tuned to a national news channel.

The clerk wasn't at the desk when they entered so

she rang the bell on the counter. "He's not still outside, is he?"

"I'll be right back."

Brock left the office and returned within a few minutes. "Nope." Then he noted, "Look, a camera."

Gisella spotted the one he was talking about. "It covers the office area." She walked back to the door, opened it and looked up. "No camera here, but—" her eyes scanned the side of the building "—there, at the end. That one's covering the parking lot."

"That's the one we need."

Brock's phone rang. When he glanced at it, he groaned. "I'll just take this outside."

"I'll talk to our guy whenever he puts in an appearance."

A door opened and Gisella spotted the hotel clerk coming from the restroom, wiping his hands on a paper towel. He pulled up short when he saw her, then offered a hard smile. Adjusting his name tag, he asked, "Can I help you with something?" He continued drying his hands. Then finally folded the paper towel into a perfect square before throwing it into the trash can next to the sofa.

"We need to look at your security camera footage," Gisella said.

"Of the parking lot, huh?"

"That would be the one," Gisella agreed with a straight face.

"Well…" He scratched his head then smoothed his

hair back into place. "I hate to tell you this, but that camera's broken. Haven't gotten around to fixing it yet."

Gisella blew out a sigh. "You've got to be kidding me."

Steve's lips twisted into a frown. "I don't kid about stuff like that, lady." His eyes narrowed into a cold stare and Gisella stared back. What was it with the people in this town?

"Fine," she muttered. "Thanks." For nothing. Walking back outside, she saw the crowd had dispersed for the most part. She stepped up to Brock and the sheriff and told them, "No security video. The camera's broken."

"Of course it is." Brock pursed his lips and shook his head.

"I think our hotel clerk has a touch of OCD."

"Obsessive Compulsive Disorder. Yeah. I noticed that too."

"Not that it matters. All right," Gisella rubbed her hands together to warm them. "I guess we can't solve everything tonight." She looked at the sheriff. "I assume you call in the forensic people from El Paso when you have something like this happen?"

He gave her an incredulous look and the red returned to his face. "Ranger, we ain't never *had* anything like this happen before."

She felt the heat rise into her cheeks. "Right. Well, I'll just give some folks in El Paso a ring and ask them to come out and go over this scene. I want it examined in detail before morning."

The sheriff lost a bit of his indignation and gave a tired sigh. "Fine. I don't blame you. I'll post Chris on it tonight until your people get here. He's got the night shift." He shot her a look. "Not that we've really needed someone to do the night shift around here."

Until now.

She heard the unspoken words as clearly as if he'd shouted them.

He rubbed his gloved hands together and continued almost to himself, "I mean, we have the occasional drunk and disorderly, illegals attempting to cross the border, but this…" He broke off and shook his head.

"I appreciate your willingness to work with us," she murmured. She looked at Brock. "It's going to be a long night."

He raised a brow. "You think?"

SIX

Four hours later, after the crime scene team from El Paso finished their examination of the car and the surrounding area, Gisella made her way back to her room to crash onto the bed. She'd left Brock on the phone with an irate boss.

Snickering, she wondered if he'd get a fourth car.

Then she sobered as she lay there staring at the ceiling, listening to the semiquiet that had finally descended upon the parking lot.

She prayed to sleep without dreams.

Surprisingly enough, she must have drifted off because the next thing she knew was the knock on the door that pulled her from the dregs of sleep. Groaning, she stumbled to the window and pushed aside the curtain.

Brock.

Of course it was. Who else would it be? He waved at her and she jerked back.

Grimacing, she ran a hand through her hair, doing her best to detangle it.

Opening the door, she looked at him and frowned. "What?"

"You don't use a peephole, either?"

"No, too easy for someone to put a bullet in my head that way."

He smiled, a slow curve to his lips that made her nerves jump and her heart stutter. "I have the same philosophy." With a glance at his watch, he said, "It's nine o'clock. You ready to get moving on this case?"

"You've got transportation?"

His lips quirked. "It should be delivered within the next twenty minutes."

"I'll be ready in twenty minutes."

She shut the door and headed for the shower.

Brock chuckled under his breath. She was definitely a beautiful woman. Spunky. Skilled and good at her job, he admitted.

Then he frowned. She still had on the clothes she'd worn yesterday. What did that mean? Had she not slept at all last night?

No, the crease on her cheek from a pillow said she had.

Huh.

Brock stood in the parking lot waiting for the vehicle his boss had reluctantly agreed to have delivered.

Brock practically had to promise the man his first-born along with assurances that he would guard the car with his life.

True to her word, Gisella was ready in just under twenty minutes. When he opened the door at her knock, Brock gave her an appreciative eye.

She sure cleaned up nice.

Actually, she looked good not cleaned up. When she'd opened the door, still fresh from sleep, she'd had an innocence about her. One that she hid from the world when she pinned that star on.

Of course she had to do that in her line of work or she'd be eaten alive. However, the impact her sleep-fogged eyes had made on his heart still lingered.

"Sleep well?" he asked, tongue in cheek.

"Shut up," she murmured with a voice sweet enough to give him a sugar high.

A low chuckle escaped him as two cars pulled into the parking lot. One for Gisella and him. And one to transport the delivery guy back to El Paso.

After the exchange of keys and a warning of dire consequences should anything happen to this latest vehicle, Gisella and Brock climbed in and drove to the little diner where they'd eaten the evening before.

Brock said, "I want to do a little observing."

"And I want to do a little questioning. Think I'll get any answers?"

He gave a shrug. "We can only try."

Brock drove the two miles to the diner and parked in front. Climbing out, they walked inside and found the same young waitress, Krista, from the night before, waiting tables. The place was filling up as they sat down.

Krista approached, no pen or pad in sight. She set two glasses of water in front of them and asked, "What can I get for you two this morning?"

Brock raised a brow. "Good morning, Krista. How about...the special?"

"That's what I would recommend," she agreed, keeping her expression pleasant in spite of her eyes dancing with mirth. She'd caught on quick to the fact that he'd been studying the sign that said, *Serving the breakfast special ONLY, this a.m. Two eggs, bacon, pancakes and grits for $6.95.*

Gisella laughed. "Make that two specials and a bottomless pot of coffee. I know I need it."

Krista started to turn away when Gisella asked, "Not that it's really any of my business, but why aren't you in school?"

"Pop needed me again." Sadness flickered in her blue eyes. "The teachers are good about letting me help him out when he needs me. Last night old man Jamison up on Three Circle Road died so Pop had to go declare him officially dead."

Gisella blinked. "Your Pop had to do that? What about the coroner?"

Krista shrugged. "He is the coroner for about six

different counties. Boot Hill is just where he happens to live."

"What?" Brock nearly choked on his sip of water.

"Yep." Krista beamed. "He was elected last year. My mom's his assistant. She actually went to school to work on bodies. She was a funeral director back in El Paso, but when she married my dad, they moved here to be near Pop and Ma. So, Mom cleans up dead people and prepares them for burial after Pop declares them dead." She shuddered and grimaced. "Which I think is just totally gross, but don't tell her that." She shot a look toward the kitchen. "Anyway, they've been busy a lot lately," she said with a sad frown. "People turning up dead all the time it seems like." Switching gears, she said, "Hey, I hear y'all had some trouble at the hotel last night."

"Yes, we did."

She shook her head and gave a disgusted sigh. "I hate that. This town's gotten so stinking unfriendly over the last couple of years. At least that's what I hear some of the older folks saying." Another subtle lift of a slender shoulder. "I don't know why. I just love having strangers stop in. Especially strangers like y'all." She wrinkled her nose and gave Brock a smile. "Keeps life from being totally boring." She grinned. "I'll be right back."

Gisella drew in a breath. "She's a teenager?"

Brock laughed as he watched the young waitress. "She does seem older, doesn't she?"

"Well, she's not, so you might want to keep that in mind."

He frowned at her. Did she really think he was that low?

Before he could ask, Gisella said, "I'm sorry, that was uncalled for. Even though she was flirting with you, you did nothing to encourage it."

The heat in her cheeks mollified him.

Krista stopped at two more tables before disappearing into the back with their order. The other waitress handled the patrons at the rear of the restaurant, casting a casual glance in their direction every so often. Brock smiled at her and she looked away in a hurry.

Huh. Interesting. That wasn't the effect he usually had on women. They usually went out of their way to get his attention. Not that it was something he was necessarily proud of—that's just the way it was.

Except for Gisella. She didn't seem the least bit susceptible to his charm. And yet he could tell she was attracted to him. A fact that sent his heart pounding with gladness and his gut churning with anxiety. When it came to women, that was a new emotion for him.

He looked back at the woman who'd intrigued him from the moment they'd met. She busied herself with drinking her water. "What do you think about the fact that Pop not only owns this restaurant but is also the coroner?"

"I think that's small-town doings for you." She gave him a half smile. "In a town like Boot Hill, the coroner is here to declare one thing. 'This person is dead.' And trust me, even though he might not have any medical experience, his word rules."

"Yeah, I know you're right. It just seems weird, that's all. I guess I've been in the city so much lately, I've forgotten what the small-town stuff is like."

"Did you grow up in a small town?" she asked.

"No. I grew up in El Paso. But lived in a small town for almost a year doing undercover work."

Her brow shot north. "Undercover? For a year? Wow. What did your family think of that?"

He gave a humorless smirk. "They didn't like it much, especially..." Breaking off, he wondered what he was doing. He never said much about the ex-fiancée, who'd refused to wait for him to finish the assignment. By the time he'd closed the case and come home, she'd moved on with someone else.

Elaine hadn't even bothered with a Dear John letter. At that point, Brock realized relationships might not be for him and had closed off that section of his heart. Or so he thought.

And yet, here he was getting ready to spill his guts about everything to a perfect stranger. A beautiful perfect stranger. One he'd already developed a lot of respect for. Even though he still thought the powers-that-be were crazy for sending her into this situation alone.

"Especially who?"

"Never mind." She didn't need to know the details. He didn't want to rehash it anyway. "It's not important. Suffice it to say, they didn't like it."

She studied him, her expression clearly saying she didn't believe for a minute that it wasn't important. But she didn't push it. Instead, she asked, "What's your family like?"

"Awfully nosey, aren't you?"

Her cheeks went rosy and a glint that could be anger entered her eyes. "I'm supposed to trust you with my life. Is it wrong for me to want to know a little about the guy I'm relying on?"

No, it wasn't wrong. In fact, she had every right to know more.

He looked away from that dark gaze that seemed to have direct access to his inner being and struggled to form an appropriate reply. "My parents are great. I don't see them much because of the job, but when we get together, it's good. I have one sister who's married with four kids." His lips twisted. "Now that's what I call a dangerous occupation."

Gisella laughed and Brock relished the sound.

"You should do that more often," he murmured.

She blushed. Clearing her throat, she glanced at him from the corner of her eye. A glance that could be interpreted as flirtatious, but he didn't think she meant it that way.

Did she?

He opened his mouth to continue, but before he could finish his spiel and reciprocate with questions, he noticed Krista on her way back from the kitchen, an overflowing plate in each hand.

The other waitress, a plain-looking girl in her mid-twenties, stopped Krista and said something. A frown crossed Krista's face but she nodded. Krista's coworker cast them another glance then ducked her head as she made her way to the next table.

Krista set their plates in front of them. "Enjoy." She spun on her heel and took off back toward the kitchen. Brock inhaled a lungful of the delicious aromas, picked up his fork and dug in. Spearing the fluffy scrambled eggs with his fork, he dipped it in the butter-laden grits. "I'll say this for small towns, they sure know good food…." He broke off when he saw Gisella had her eyes closed.

A few seconds later, she opened them. He flushed and said, "Sorry."

"No problem. Just saying a short grace. I didn't mean to embarrass you."

Before he could respond that he wasn't embarrassed by the prayer, but his own thoughtlessness, Krista returned to refill their water and coffee cups.

Glancing behind her, she leaned closer and almost

whispered. "Ina, the other waitress, wants to know if you're here investigating the drug smuggling that goes on around here."

Brock straightened, eyes locked on the young girl. "Yes, we are. What do you know about that?"

She shrugged, reached out and knocked a glass off the table. "Oh! I'm so sorry!"

Kneeling, the girl cast a worried glance in the direction of the men in the corner then whispered, "Nothing, except I overheard some people talking about you. And I may be young, but even I know the smuggling is going on all the time." She focused on wiping up the rest of the water. In a normal tone of voice, she said, "I'll be right back with another glass for you."

Krista carried the empty glass and wet towel back toward the kitchen.

"She meant to knock that glass off," Brock said.

"That's what I thought, too. She was covering up the fact that she wanted to talk to us."

"She also already had that large towel in preparation to clean up the spill."

Gisella looked at him, impressed. "Yes, she did."

Krista returned with a fresh glass and placed it on the table in front of Gisella. "I have a friend who wants to talk to you, but she can't be seen with you. She said to wait for her to contact you but needs your number."

Without another word, she grabbed a couple of their empty plates and sauntered off toward the kitchen. Brock watched Gisella discreetly scan the area behind them. Lifting her coffee cup to her lips, she murmured, "The other waitress is being watched by the three men in the corner booth. And so are we."

"You think they might be a good place to start the questioning?"

"Definitely."

Brock pulled out his wallet and placed a few bills on the table along with his card that had his cell phone number on it. "Hopefully, Krista will pass that on to her friend." He finished off his coffee. "So, how are you at ambushing unsuspecting old men?"

Gisella grinned, took another sip of her water and stood. "I'm ready to find out."

She slipped from the booth and headed to the three men who seemed to take such an interest in her and Brock's presence.

As she approached, they fell quiet and watched her. One raised a bushy gray brow and another gulped a swallow of soda. The third one simply narrowed his eyes.

Gisella slipped an easy smile on her lips and said, "Good morning. I'm Ranger Gisella Hernandez and this is my partner, Brock Martin, with the DEA. How are y'all doing?"

She got two nods and one howdy from the eldest of the trio. He looked to be at least ninety years old with only four or five teeth left in his mouth. In a voice long abused probably by cigarettes if the unlit one he let dangle from his lips was any indication, he rasped, "Guess you noticed us watching ya, huh?"

"I did. Which led me to believe you might be open to answering a few questions."

"We were watching you, but it wasn't because we wanted to answer any questions," snarled the youngest of the trio, a man in his early thirties. His lip curled and he crossed his arms across his chest as he looked Gisella up and down in a way that sent ripples of disgust through her. "We got law enforcement in this town. Don't need no uppity Ranger and her sidekick coming along stirring things up."

From the corner of her eye, she glimpsed Brock's hand curling into a fist. Gisella squinted and kept her voice pleasant. "I've met your sheriff and one of his deputies. They seem quite competent. And I promise I'm not trying to 'stir' anything up. Drugs are coming in across the border at a rapid rate. We're just trying to do our best to help keep your town safe."

The man's lip didn't uncurl.

His buddy next to him, one who looked to be in his early forties, had on a plaid shirt and a cowboy hat that had seen better days. She could smell it from where she stood.

However, he looked like he might be less hostile toward her. She addressed her question to him. "I need to know if you know of anyone with the initials JZ."

The oldest man lifted a hand to rub his stubbled chin. "JZ. Can't think of anyone right off with those initials. Sorry."

The other two shook their heads in unison.

"What about RP and QV?" Brock asked.

"Well, there's Ruben Perez," the youngest one offered. "He's the pastor out at the little church along Triple Spur Road." He gave a snicker. "Can't see him having nothing to do with anything that might require a hotshot like you to come after him."

Gisella nodded and noted the name then offered a friendly smile. "Glad to hear it. Thanks for the name. If you think of anyone else, would you give me a call?" She pulled a card from her pocket and handed one to each man. The eldest of the trio looked to be the most open, eyeing her and Brock with curiosity, an amused glint in his gaze.

Interesting. Not one of them had bothered with an introduction. "Could we get your names in case we have any more questions?"

The surly young one stood. "You're the Ranger, you figure it out." He stomped from the restaurant.

The old geezer chuckled. "Aw, don't mind him.

Jasper's a might testy lately. Been trying to keep the coyotes off his land. They're getting braver every year."

Coyotes, she wondered. Or was he involved in something else that gave him a nasty attitude toward law enforcement?

She registered the name. "Does Jasper have a last name?"

A flush darkened his face as he gave a tug on the smelly cowboy hat. "Jasper West. I'm Clarence Ponder."

"And I'm Carlos Ortez."

Gisella gave a nod. "Well, gentlemen, thank you very much for talking to us. I'm sure we'll be in touch should we need anything."

Clarence winked at her and gave her a close-to-toothless grin. "I might be able to think of something if it means getting to talk to you again, pretty lady."

Gisella felt the flush rise into her neck and cleared her throat. "Thank you, Mr. Ponder."

Five minutes later, they had directions to the little church where Ruben Perez was the pastor.

Stepping outside the restaurant, Gisella paused and looked at the small town's main street. "You know, if not for the cars, this place could pass for an old Western town from back in the day."

"Definitely," he murmured.

He was listening, but not to her. Gisella's senses

immediately sharpened and the hair on the back of her neck snapped to attention. "What is it?"

"I feel like someone's watching us."

She gave a light snort. "I've felt that way since we got here."

"Yeah, me, too. But this is more. It's like the calm before the storm. Eerie and silent, and then bam, it hits."

She shivered. "Okay, now you're starting to spook me."

He didn't smile. "Call it instinct after years of being a cop and now DEA. It's the same feeling I had when Lenny pulled that gun on me. Only I didn't listen to it then. I'm listening now."

"Then we need to be extra careful," she muttered.

"Why don't we head over to the church and see if the pastor is there? What he has to say will determine our next steps."

"And let's watch our backs as we go."

SEVEN

"Come in."

Pastor Ruben Perez opened his office door and beckoned them to enter. Fortunately, the part-time secretary had been in her office when Brock called and asked to see the pastor. He'd been waiting for them.

Perez slipped behind his desk and asked, "What can I do for you?"

Brock held the door for Gisella. As she stepped inside, her shoulder brushed his chest and he caught his breath. Being so close to her did strange things to his pulse. Not that he'd never been attracted to a woman before, but he'd never been attracted to someone like Gisella. One who understood his job for starters. One who didn't let him intimidate her. And one who wasn't attracted to him because she thought cops were glamorous.

Very strange.

But was it worth the possible heartache of pursuing?

Gisella sat in the rickety wooden chair and it

wobbled. She caught herself and the pastor flushed. "Sorry, we're a poor church and…" He spread his hands in a helpless gesture. "I thought *mi hermano,* my brother, had fixed that thing." He stood. "Here, take mine."

"No, it's fine." She perched carefully and smiled at the man. Brock watched the pastor relax under the influence of her charm.

He paused. Is that what he was doing? Falling for her charm? Maybe. He raised his guard a bit.

She said, "Thank you for seeing us on such short notice."

"No problemo." He gave a shrug and Brock judged him to be in his early forties. A tall man who easily topped six feet, he exuded a sincerity that Brock found intriguing.

She leaned forward. "We're here investigating reports of drug runners in the area and wondered if you might be able to tell us anything."

The pastor held up a hand. "I don't get involved in that stuff. I know that some members of my congregation are. However, we have a don't ask, don't tell policy."

Gisella frowned. "Is that safe?"

Ruben sighed and rubbed his cheek. "It is the only way I can build a relationship with the people here. I am not from here originally, therefore I'm still considered an outsider. However—" he lifted a finger for emphasis "—after seven years, they are beginning to trust me, allowing me into their homes, permitting me to help them and to pray for them."

"Very admirable," Brock interjected, "but your initials were found in a book that has information about drug running here in Boot Hill." Okay, so they didn't exactly know that the RP in the book had anything to do with the man in front of him, but why come out and say so?

"My initials?" A black brow shot south. "What made you assume the letters referred to me?"

Gisella shot Brock an irritated look. "We didn't just assume that, Pastor Perez. However, when we asked around as to who the initials could belong to, your name came up."

"Ah." He nodded. "I see. Well, I can assure you I have nothing to do with the drug running. I am doing my best to stop it, too." He smiled. "I just use prayers and love instead of guns."

Brock's phone buzzed. He looked at the number and didn't recognize it. Excusing himself, he stepped outside the office and took the call. "Martin."

Silence.

"Hello?" he barked.

"Um…are you the one who wants information about the people involved in the drugs?" Brock barely made out the words; the whisper was almost nonexistent, but he thought it sounded like a young woman.

"Yes, who is this?" He thought it was probably the girl from the restaurant. Ina something.

"Could you meet me tonight? Will you pay me for information?"

He snatched the opportunity. "Sure, where do you want to meet?"

"The graveyard on the east end of town."

His stomach clenched. "Why there?"

"I want to show you something. You have to see to understand."

"See what?"

"I won't tell you until I have the money, but you will be glad you came."

"Fine. I'll be there. What time?"

"Nine o'clock. You bring the money, too?" Her voice wavered as though unsure whether or not to ask.

He went along. "How much?"

"One, no, two hundred dollars. *Sí,* two hundred."

An amateur. She hadn't thought this all out. She'd sounded sure about the meeting place and time, but not the amount of money. Was it an impulse idea to sell the information?

"This better be some good stuff."

"*Sí,* very good, I promise."

Brock hung up the phone as Gisella and the pastor exited the office.

He waved the phone at her. "We have another appointment."

Curiosity lit her eyes, but she didn't ask. Instead, she said to Ruben, "Thank you for talking to us. If you can think of anything that might help us, just give us a call."

"I have your card. I will do so."

Back in the car, Brock filled her in on the conversation he'd just had. She glanced at her watch. "It's not even noon yet. I want to go out to the border crossing and talk to some of the agents, however, I really feel like if we focus on the information in that book, it's going to blow this drug smuggling case wide open."

"So, the border? Or the hotel?"

Gisella blew out a sigh. "I guess the hotel for now. We can study the book for a bit and if we don't come up with something, we can make our way over to the border crossing. It's not far from here and I want to get out there soon."

Brock turned toward the hotel. "Sounds like a great plan."

She leaned her head back against the headrest. "I don't know. With the book, I just keep hoping something's going to jump out at us."

Brock snorted. "Right." Then he looked at her and shrugged. "Why not?"

He wouldn't mind spending a little time with her. He wanted to ask her some personal questions but didn't want to put her on her guard with him—any more than she already was. That he wanted to get to know her bothered him.

A lot of things about her bothered him.

Like the fact that he thought she might be the first woman since his ex-fiancée that he could actually find himself caring about.

The little sliver of fear that darted through him shook him.

To the core.

Putting his heart back out there would take a courage he wasn't sure he had. He thought he might prefer facing armed drug runners.

"Are you okay?"

He jerked and looked at her. "Oh. Yeah. Fine. Why?"

She wrinkled her nose at him. "I don't know. Something seems to be bothering you."

Hoping his year-round tan hid the flush he could feel working its way up the back of his neck, he gave a nonchalant shrug. "Sorry, just thinking about how we're going to figure out where those drugs are coming from. I really do think we're on to something here."

"I agree."

He pulled into the hotel parking lot and he noticed the scene from last night was gone. Except for the charred area of the asphalt, no one would suspect anything out of the ordinary had happened the night before.

Climbing out, she asked, "You want to meet in the conference room if it's available? I think I saw a sign that said they had Wi-Fi there."

Brock shook his head. "I wouldn't have thought this place would be that technologically advanced."

"I didn't say it worked. I said I saw a sign."

He gave a low chuckle, appreciating her dry humor. "If it doesn't, I have a broadband card."

"Although, I have to say, for a small town, this hotel has really surprised me."

"I'm with you there."

"I'll get my computer and see you in a few—" She came to the door to her room and stopped, reached for her weapon and motioned for him to do the same.

"What is it?" he whispered. Stepping up behind her, he froze. Her door was cracked. Mimicking her actions, he reached for his gun.

From the side, she toed the door open. It swung in without a sound. Odd. This morning it had groaned like an old man getting out of bed.

Brock stood opposite her, his stance saying he was ready. In one smooth move, she rounded the door jam and pointed her weapon.

Into an empty room.

One that had been ransacked. Pillows lay on the floor, her bag had been tossed, her cell phone charger pulled from the wall. She wondered if her laptop was still under the mattress.

Brock tread on silent feet to her left, then ahead

of her. He cocked his head to the bathroom. She nodded and slipped to the bathroom door.

Crouching, she peered around the door and aimed her gun into the small area. Brock followed, weapon held ready. He swung around the entrance to aim at the tub.

Gisella pulled in a deep breath and shot a glance at Brock. The shower curtain had been pulled shut. She always left it open. Stepping into the bathroom to check behind the curtain could sign her death warrant.

She held up a finger to Brock in a signal to wait. Silently lifting herself to her feet, she stepped back into the room and grabbed a pillow from the bed.

Back at the entrance to the bathroom, standing off to the side so if someone decided to shoot she wouldn't be a target, she slung the pillow blindly at the shower curtain. She heard it drop into the tub with a thud. A quick glance around the door showed the shower curtain fluttering. No one waited behind it.

Gisella felt her muscles relax. "Clear."

Brock lowered his gun and blew out a sigh. "Clear."

Holstering her weapon, she asked, "What do you think about that message?"

He got to his feet and walked into the bathroom to grab a towel. Using it, he pulled the curtain back and together they examined the writing that glared back at them.

"Leave or Die," she read.

EIGHT

"Well," Brock said, "it tells us one thing. We're in the right place, asking the right questions."

"And stirring things up."

"Which you said you weren't going to do," he reminded her, tongue in cheek.

Shooting him a look that said he wasn't funny, she sighed. "I don't suppose it's worth calling the forensics team back here from El Paso, is it?"

Brock rubbed his chin as he studied the writing. "I don't think so. You and I can gather the evidence as well as any team. The car was a little beyond my abilities, but this… I have a camera in my car. Let me get some pictures."

"What about a fingerprint kit?"

Raising a brow, he asked, "There's probably five thousand different prints in this bathroom. You don't think that would be a waste of time?"

"I don't know," she murmured. "This place was pretty clean when we checked in. It had been scrubbed down. I'm thinking it might be worth a shot."

Brock shrugged. "All right, I'll bring the fingerprint kit, too. When my car was dropped off, it should have been equipped with everything I had in the other one." Looking around, he frowned.

She noticed. "What?"

"Whoever did this took the evidence with him."

"Is it spray paint?"

"I think so. Doesn't look like it was brushed on." He leaned in closer, lips pursed. "Yeah, definitely sprayed." With a gloved finger, he touched it then looked at the glove. "And dry. It was probably done shortly after we left the hotel."

"So, where's the can? Is that what you're thinking?"

"Mmm-hmm."

She didn't like the look in his eye. Warily, she questioned, "Where are you thinking of looking for that can?"

A smile started at one corner of his lips. He really did have beautiful lips. She blinked and focused on what he was saying.

"Exactly where you're thinking I'm thinking."

She groaned, her brief romantic thoughts dissolving like fog in the morning sun. "Ugh. I hope you've got some extra sets of gloves in that well-equipped car of yours. Dumpster diving is definitely my least favorite sport."

"Weak stomach?" He smirked.

Narrowing her eyes at him, she gave a tight smile.

"What, you think a woman can't handle a dirty job like that?"

False innocence radiated from him. "Hey, I didn't say that."

"Right." Gisella snorted and walked to the main door of the room. All bantering aside, she examined the hinges. "This door creaked like an old rocker this morning when we left. Now suddenly, it opens without a sound."

He handed her a tissue and she swiped the top hinge. A substance with a brown tint appeared on the surface. "Oil."

Brock looked over her shoulder. Once again his cologne wafted to her nose and she inhaled it for probably the tenth time that day. She seemed to do that a lot around him. Flushing, she concentrated on the task at hand. "So, who oiled the door? And why? Because it simply needed it?"

"Or because someone wanted to make sure if he entered you wouldn't hear him?"

"I don't like that last possibility."

"Neither do I." His breath wafted against her cheek and she realized how close he was standing.

Curling her gloved fingers around the oil-stained tissue, she asked, "Why don't you get that stuff from the car so I can bag this?"

"Yes, ma'am, why don't I do just that?" He shot her a knowing smile and Gisella felt her flush burn hotter.

She watched him leave and couldn't help admiring

the breadth of his shoulders and the way his clothes looked like they'd been made just for him. He wore them well.

Her cell phone rang and she snatched it from the clip on her side. "Gisella here."

"Gisella, this is Ben. How's it going down there in Boot Hill? Are you making any progress?"

Ben Fritz, her captain.

"Hi, Ben." She blew out a sigh. "Well, from the looks of my hotel room, it's obvious we're making someone uncomfortable." She quickly brought him up to date. "I really think we're in the right spot. Give me a few more days and I'll probably have more to tell you."

"You got it. Just keep me updated. And let me know if and when you need some backup. I can send Levi or Evan." Levi McDonnell and Evan Chen. Two other Rangers in her company.

Gisella thanked him. "I think Brock and I've got it covered for now. Once we find out who's trying to get us to leave town, I think we'll find a lead to the drugs. We'll be heading over to the border crossing pretty soon. We just have to take care of a few things first."

"Sounds good. Talk to you soon."

Gisella hung up as Brock walked back into the room with his supplies. "I think we should check your room."

He nodded. "I thought about that."

"But I don't want to leave this scene unsecured."

"I'll holler if I need help. My guess is our guy is long gone. The dried spray paint tells me that much."

She blew out a breath. "You're probably right. Still, I'll stand outside the door while you check your room."

He set the supplies on the floor and they exited the room. Brock went to his door and nudged it with his elbow. It stayed put.

Pulling out his key, he swiped it and with a glove-covered hand turned the knob. Standing off to the side, he gave the door a shove and it swung in.

When nothing happened, he peered around into the room.

And relaxed. Still, she knew he wouldn't call it clear until he'd checked the bathroom. Still keeping an eye on her own door, she crept closer to his.

"Clear!" he called.

She took her hand from her weapon and stepped back into her room. He followed and said, "No one there. Doesn't even look like someone tried to get in."

"So, they're picking on me, huh?"

He quirked a smile. "Looks like it." Then he turned to the kit. "Now let's see what we can find so we can get the little weasel."

Bit by bit, they processed the room. She snapped pictures while he gathered, bagged and dusted.

When she felt she'd gotten all the photos she could use, she helped him finish up. She held up a large bag. "Just a guess, but I think it's useless to hope anything is going to come off this shower curtain."

He agreed and stood. "Ready for the fun part?"

She grimaced. "Sure."

Brock had to admit the woman had grit. Digging through nasty Dumpsters wasn't his favorite part of the job either. You never knew what you were going to come across. However, it had to be done.

And it would be fun to watch her wrinkle her nose as she went about doing it. He didn't have a ladder so he'd have to improvise.

Pulling the car up to the Dumpster, he got out and climbed on the hood, doing his best not to leave any dents. To Gisella's credit, she simply raised a brow and kept any comments to herself.

Snapping a clean pair of gloves on, he leaned over the edge of the bin. "You coming?"

"Right behind you." Placing a foot on the front bumper, she hauled herself up, keeping to the edge of the car. "Wouldn't it have been a lot easier to ask for a ladder?"

"Probably."

He thought he heard her chuckle under her breath but figured she'd bite off her tongue before admitting it. He peered over the edge and examined the contents. He sighed. "Not this one."

"How do you know?" She gave an indignant snort. "You're not going digging?"

"No way. The suspect would have tossed the can and kept going."

She shot him a wry look. "Or didn't bother with the toss and just kept going."

"Taking the evidence with him. Yeah, yeah." He looked around. "But on the off chance he didn't…"

"Over there." She pointed to the other bin next to the end of the building.

Brock maneuvered the car next to that one and Gisella climbed up this time. "Bingo," she grunted and reached in.

"You found it?"

Had she really or was she playing with him?

"Yep."

"I can't believe it was that easy."

His regret must have shown clearly on his face because she gave a small laugh and asked, "Why? Were you hoping I'd have to get all smelly?"

He winced. "Definitely not." Then he gave her a slow smile. "I like the perfume you have on now as opposed to Eau du Dumpster. Makes me think of things like roses and candles."

The flush that popped out on her olive-toned cheeks made him grin. She hopped down, an empty can of red spray paint in her left gloved hand. With a glare that was in direct contrast to her heated complexion, she raised a brow. He kept the smile as he held open a bag.

Dropping the evidence in, she didn't comment on his obvious flirtation. Instead she said, "We'll definitely send that off to El Paso. I'm guessing our vandal didn't have gloves on when he bought it. Maybe there'll be a print."

Brock let her change the subject. He probably shouldn't be flirting with her anyway. Not if he didn't want his heart to get broken into a million pieces. "I have a friend in the lab. I'll make a call and get an answer asap."

Drily, she asked, "What's her name?"

"What do you mean?" He gave her that innocent look again but before he could respond further, a voice asked, "What's going on out here?"

Their attention from their evidence, Brock gave a grim smile while Gisella tossed her braid over her left shoulder. "Hello, Sheriff."

"What are you two up to now?"

Gisella pulled her gloves off and tossed them into the Dumpster. Planting her hands on her hips, she said, "Someone broke into my room. We just finished processing it."

His brow rose and his jaw firmed. "You didn't think to give me a call?"

Brock broke in. "There wasn't any reason to bother you with it right away. We took care of it."

The man's eyes narrowed. "Now look here, this is

my town. I'm responsible for all that goes on here. And that means knowing when a crime occurs."

Gisella nodded. "And we were going to report it, we just thought we'd take care of processing it first."

"That's what you thought, huh?" Sheriff Johnston shook his head and sighed. "So, did you find anything?"

"An almost empty can of spray paint." Brock held up the bag.

The big man blew out a sigh and hitched his pants. "All right. We'll send it off and see if we get any prints off it."

"That's what we planned," Brock agreed. "You wouldn't happen to know which store might sell this, would you?" He held the bag so the man could look in.

"Hank's Hardware is my guess. Two streets over, third building on the right." The sheriff shrugged. "But it could have come from a couple different places."

"Or another town," Gisella said. "There's no guarantee it was bought here. Or even bought since we got here. Someone could have had it sitting in his garage and decided to put it to use here."

"True." Brock showed the evidence to the sheriff. "I'm going to send this off for processing. I'll let you know what we learn."

Gisella eyed Sheriff Johnston. "Did you have something you needed?"

"Nah. Old man Grueber said he saw someone digging through the trash over here and I told him I'd check it out." He headed back toward his car. Over his shoulder, he said, "Y'all stay outta trouble." Then he stopped and turned back. "Seriously, if you need anything, give me a call, would you? It's my job."

Gisella offered him a small smile. "Sure thing, Sheriff."

With a shake of his head, he climbed in his car and sped away. Gisella looked at Brock and shrugged. "Okay, let's get this evidence shipped off then get a map of the graveyard and figure out a plan to meet this informant."

NINE

Hours later, Gisella sat in the car, staring out the window into the dark night, thinking about the man beside her. He exuded strength and intelligence and a cockiness she found charming…and occasionally irritating. But the flashes of vulnerability he'd allowed her to see intrigued her, made her realize there was more to Brock Martin than met the eye.

She'd known him for all of two days and the initial zing of attraction she'd felt hadn't faded. That worried her. And excited her. She'd thought about getting married, of course; what woman hadn't? And yet, she'd been so consumed with her job, she hadn't bothered to even find the time to date someone.

She longed to talk things over with her friend, Corinna, but hadn't had a moment to make a phone call. Corinna was Captain Gregory Pike's daughter. She had found his body in their home. His killer had yet to be found.

Which was why Gisella was meeting a possible

informant in a dark graveyard. She nearly smiled at the drama of it all. Then frowned. Why the grave-yard?

When Brock pulled into a spot under a tree at the entrance to the cemetery, she glanced at her watch. 8:30.

A streetlamp at the entrance cast a weak glow onto the walkway. Earlier, she and Brock had driven over to get a feel for the graveyard's layout and had picked the best place to park and wait. He shut the car off and soon the cold from outside began to permeate the interior.

"So your caller didn't specify a meeting spot?" she asked.

"No." He grabbed his bottle of water from the cup holder and took a swig. "She just said to meet her at the graveyard at 9:00."

"Weird."

"Agreed."

Gisella chewed her lip as she thought. "She said she had something to show you, right?"

"Yes."

"Wonder what she meant by that? I mean it's one thing to need to *tell* someone something, quite another to *show* someone something. You know what I mean?"

Brock gave a slow nod. "You're right. But she definitely said, 'show,' not tell." He paused. "I'm ninety-nine percent sure it's Ina from the restaurant, but I didn't want to scare her off by letting on I knew who she was." He looked at her. "While we're waiting, why don't you tell me how—and why—you got into this line of work?"

Gisella sucked in a breath. She'd known that question would be asked sooner or later. Apparently, the time was now. "A lot of different reasons."

"You mind sharing them?" His hand settled on her shoulder and she jumped—then stilled under the warmth of his touch. It made her nervous that she liked it.

That she liked *him*.

Really liked him.

In spite of her initial judgment of him after seeing him in action, getting to know him better, she had a feeling there was more to him than he let on. She wanted to probe those depths and figure out what made him tick.

"My brother died of an overdose when I was sixteen," she said softly. "He was eighteen."

He drew in a swift breath. "Wow."

"Yeah. Wow."

He remained silent, letting her go at her own pace. She brushed at her pant leg and adjusted her badge. "We were at a party. I followed him when he snuck out of the house." She shot him a wry look. "And yes, he was sneaking out of the house at eighteen. If you knew my parents, you would understand that it was better to sneak out than face the inquisition."

Brock nodded. "I get it. The old 'You live under my roof, you follow my rules' dictatorship?"

"Oh, yeah. Totally." She shrugged. "When José realized I'd followed him, he was furious. But there wasn't much he could do about it. So he basically ignored me while I watched him drink. Then—" she pulled in a deep breath "—he started snorting the white powder."

"Cocaine." He spat the word as though it left a vile taste in his mouth.

"Cocaine," she confirmed. "I couldn't believe it. Our father had told us stories of how he used to fight the drug war and here my brother was putting that stuff in his body." Gisella swallowed at the memory. "There was absolutely nothing I could do about it short of calling the cops and I sure wasn't doing that. So I watched. And then he was on the ground. Twitching. Clutching his chest."

Her voice shook and she bit her lip. "I ran to him. Screamed at someone to call for help." A slow shake of her head shifted her braid. She absently shoved it back. "But it was too late. No one wanted an ambulance there with all the drugs laying around. I grabbed a cell phone out of someone's hand and dialed 911. But it was too late. He was dead before I finished punching in the numbers." A tear slipped down her cheek before she could stop it. She swiped it away, hoping he hadn't seen it and clenched her jaw. "I decided then and there I'd get rid of as many drug dealers as I could. And I have. More than any *man* in my department." The taunt was soft, without heat.

He gave a small smile. "Your family must be proud."

Surprised at the continued sting of tears, she blinked them back, refusing to allow another one to fall, and looked into the night.

Automatically she scanned the area. Seeing nothing, she shrugged. "You would think. But no. They're not happy with my chosen profession. My dad was a Ranger and is on me all the time about the danger."

Brock jerked. "No way."

"Why?"

"My dad was, too. What company?"

She told him. He laughed and shook his head. "I wonder if they know each other."

"It's possible, I suppose."

Looking at her, he ran a finger down her cheek and she shivered. He studied her and she let him. "You're very beautiful, you know that?" Then he seemed to withdraw mentally. Placing his hand back on the wheel, he drew in a deep breath. "So what do you do when you're not chasing bad guys?"

Grateful for the change in topic, she breathed a little laugh. "I swim."

"No kidding?"

"Oh, come on," she scoffed. "If you say you swim, too, I'm so not going to believe you."

The hand on her shoulder squeezed. "No. I mean I can swim—as you found out when I surprised you at the pool—but I like to go at it with a punching bag to let off steam."

"What else do you like to do?"

"I play a pretty good game of racquetball."

Movement caught her eye and she leaned forward. "Hey, I think I saw something."

Instantly all business, he trained his gaze in the direction she indicated.

"Someone's sneaking through the trees," he muttered.

The shape darted from the trees to a headstone. Moving away from their vehicle.

Gisella glanced at her watch. It was almost 9. "I can't see enough to tell who it might be," she mused. "Our appointment? Or someone who shouldn't be here?"

Just then the person caught sight of their car, pulled up short, spun on a heel and took off through the cemetery. Brock and Gisella slammed out of their vehicle at the same time. Gisella yanked out her weapon just for safety's sake as Brock raced down the rocky sidewalk and into the graveyard. "Freeze! Hey, we just want to talk."

His yell bounced off the headstones around them.

Gisella cut across the other way hoping to head the man off. And it was definitely a man, his shape briefly outlined by the dim light provided by the moon.

In the darkness, Gisella could barely make out the figure she was chasing. Her foot caught on the edge of a cement marker and she stumbled. By the time she steadied herself and looked up, the man was gone.

She stood. Silent. Listening.

All she heard was her own raspy, uneven breaths. As they slowed, she tuned in to her surroundings. Partial moonlight filtered through the trees giving the area an eerie, ethereal feeling.

Gisella shivered and tugged her coat tighter around her throat. Where was Brock?

Closing her eyes, she used her ears.

Nothing sounded out of place.

Of course, how did a graveyard usually sound at night?

Quiet, no doubt.

Another shiver racked her. The temperatures were falling fast now. It had to be below freezing. She kept her glove on her left hand. Her right hand felt glued around the butt of her weapon. Not a good thing. But as long as she could still pull the trigger, she'd be all right.

Which way should she search?

She headed in the direction she thought the runner

would have most likely gone. Her feet crunched on the frozen ground and she paused.

If she made noise when she walked, she should also be able to hear anyone else's footsteps.

Her stomach twisted as she looked around. Lots of hiding places behind the tombstones.

Was he watching her even now?

If he had a gun trained on her, she was dead.

Heart picking up speed, she slipped behind a large headstone and listened.

Again, nothing.

Was he long gone by now? Or lying in wait?

And then she heard it. A slight scrape.

Brock?

Not wanting to call out, she pulled in a deep breath and peered around the corner.

A gunshot sounded, pinged off the headstone she was behind and she jerked back.

"Brock!" She grabbed her phone and punched in the sheriff's number.

Another shot. Then silence reigned.

The sheriff's phone rang. And rang. Finally, "Sheriff's office."

"This is Gisella Hernandez, Texas Ranger." She gave her location. "I'm requesting backup! Now! Shots fired!"

"The sheriff is on his way, ma'am."

Brock must have called, too. Good to know he was able. Gisella hung up and sped in the direction of the shots, taking care to keep an eye out for the shooter. Another shot sounded and ricocheted off the headstone next to her. Cement particles stung her face and she blinked as she ducked behind the marker.

A body landed beside her and she bit off the scream as she realized who it was. "Brock! I could've shot you! Give a girl some warning, will you?"

Ignoring her muttered words and black look, Brock said to her, "I've called the sheriff for backup. Are you ready?"

Still reeling from his sudden appearance, she looked at him, wariness punching through her. "Ready for what?"

"See that line of headstones?" She looked where he pointed. Several large grave markers sat side by side providing an adequate cover—assuming a bullet didn't slip through one of the spaces between them. He pointed. "I'm going that way. They'll give me some cover. When he starts shooting at me, you go around the other way and come up behind him." If she'd been able to make out his features, she was sure his jaw would be tight with that little muscle jumping along the edge of it.

"Sounds good to me. Just…don't get shot, please?"

She thought he breathed a low chuckle, then he was gone, ducking behind the headstones as he'd planned. Two more shots sounded in quick succession. Brock still didn't return fire and neither did Gisella. She wasn't going to shoot blind.

Gisella rolled to her feet and took off. The flash from the next shot told her the general area of the shooter.

Heading in that direction, careful to keep herself at least partially protected, she weaved around several headstones to slide behind a mausoleum.

Silence reigned once more.

Where was he?

No more shots had been fired.

She narrowed her eyes and listened. Not even a cricket chirped.

Had he managed to escape? He'd disappeared like smoke on the wind. Once again she scanned the area.

Where was Brock?

Not wanting to assume the shooter was gone, she kept to the shadows. Which wasn't hard in the almost total darkness of the cemetery.

A siren sounded and lights flashed in the distance.

Backup had arrived. It was about time.

She let her gaze rove from one place to the next. The trees, the headstones, the space beyond.

But spotted nothing to indicate anyone sinister lingered.

Breathing out a sigh of frustration, she looked for Brock. Where had he disappeared to? Had their fugitive managed to slip past her and into Brock's path? If so, was Brock still chasing the man? Did he need help?

Glancing back over her shoulder, she caught a glimpse of the sheriff's silhouette briefly illuminated by one of the weak lights in the graveyard.

It looked like he'd brought his deputies.

Not ready to holster her weapon yet, she walked toward the other officers, silently wondering—and worrying—about Brock.

Concern nipped at her. He hadn't been hit, had he? And what about the informant? Had all the commotion scared her off? Had she even shown up to begin with?

"Hello, Sheriff."

"What's going on out here, Ranger?" He wasn't happy, she could see it in his eyes. Well, he could join the club.

Keeping her sarcasm to herself, she stated, "We had a phone call asking us to meet an informant here at nine o'clock. We got here early. I spotted movement in the graveyard and we thought it was who we were supposed to meet." She gave a grim smile. "It wasn't. He started shooting at us. I think by the time you showed up, he was pretty much gone."

The sheriff shook his head and motioned for Deputy Chris Locke. "Go see what you can find." He looked at Niles Vernon. "You wanted to see what all the commotion was about. Well, here we are. You want to help find this guy?"

Niles shrugged. "Sure. I'll help out. We're right near the border so this is my territory anyway."

Chris headed off in the direction the sheriff indicated.

Then Johnston asked Gisella, "Where's Agent Martin?"

"The last I saw him was over in that direction." She pointed then started walking that way, keeping her eyes open and alert. She didn't want any surprises.

"Brock! Where are you?" Worry tugged at her.

"Over here." She almost didn't hear his low words to her left. She walked a few more feet and saw his head just above the edge of a large headstone.

When she stepped forward for a better view, she looked down and gasped. "Oh, no! What happened?"

"Someone didn't want her talking."

Together they stared down at the waitress's body.

TEN

Brock rubbed his neck while Pop, the coroner/restaurant owner, stated he'd take the body back to the morgue—rather, the building they used as a morgue. "It's in the back of the doctor's office. Just a small room with a freezer and an autopsy table, but good enough for this little town."

Brock and Gisella exchanged a look. "Sheriff, we need someone from El Paso to process the body."

He snorted. "And I need a month-long vacation in the Bahamas, but it doesn't look like that's going to happen, either." Then his face softened a fraction. "Look, you two have worked more than one small town. You know that's not how things are done around here."

Brock narrowed his eyes. "But it could be. It just takes a little longer."

The sheriff spread his hands and said to Brock, "Why don't you do the best you can do with her and I'll see who I can get in touch with in El Paso. I've got evidence bags in the back of my car." He went to get them and Brock followed.

Studying Ina before the coroner arrived had given Brock a few clues. She had several broken finger-nails and a cut on her lip. A bruise over her right eye suggested someone or something had hit her pretty hard. The marks around her throat indicated she'd been strangled.

Had the blow to her head knocked her out and then the killer strangled her? Or had she looked into his eyes as she took her last breath?

Questions to which he might never have answers. Sighing, he clenched his fingers into tight fists.

At the car, the sheriff opened his trunk and pulled out a small suitcase. "Everything you need should be in here."

"Sheriff," he said in his most convincing voice, "I have one of those cases in my own car. But we need a crime scene unit to process this. We also need a medical examiner to work with the body. I don't have any proof, but I strongly suspect this girl was killed because of something she was going to tell us tonight. Please, we're at your mercy. Help us out here and let those who have more training than I do come in and do what needs to be done."

The sheriff hitched his pants and rubbed a hand down his chin. He seemed to consider his options before giving a slow nod. "All right. You could be right. This is all beyond my scope of expertise. I mean, I've dealt with a few drug runners that wound up dead and the occasional domestic violence that ended badly, but this…" Shaking his head, his eyes expressed his sadness. "Ina's mama's going to be beside herself with grief."

Gisella stepped up beside them and looked at Brock. "Did you convince him that in order for Ina to have the kind of justice she needs, we really need to call in the forensic team from El Paso?"

Brock looked the sheriff in the eye. "I don't know, Sheriff. Did I?"

Although he'd just agreed a few seconds earlier, the sheriff still hesitated.

Chris appeared just in time to hear Gisella's and Brock's statements. He shot a glare in their direction. "Now look here, just because we're in a small town doesn't mean…"

"I'll call them." The sheriff cut him off with a sharp look. "They're right." Pulling out his cell phone, he punched in the appropriate numbers while Brock breathed a little easier.

"Don't forget the medical examiner," Brock reminded him. The sheriff shot him a glare that clearly said for Brock to be quiet.

Chris rolled his eyes and muttered something under his breath as he walked away. Brock made a mental note to do a background check on that guy. Something besides the man's lousy attitude bothered him.

Stepping up to Pop, Brock said, "We're having a team come from El Paso to process the body, Mr. Luc."

The coroner nodded. "It's just Angelo—or Pop. And I figured you might. I'll have her on ice. Just let me know what you need."

"Thanks." Brock didn't necessarily like the "on ice" comment, but held his tongue. "But we need to leave her where she is until the ME can get here."

The older man shrugged. "All right."

While they waited for the crime scene unit from El Paso to arrive, Brock motioned for Gisella to come over.

As she stepped next to him, the sheriff pocketed his cell phone and said, "The forensics team is on the way back from El Paso, but the medical examiner can't get out here until tomorrow sometime."

Brock blew out a breath. "Oh. That's going to mess us up a bit." He looked at Gisella. "We'll do what we can here and wait to see what the ME has to say after he gets here tomorrow."

"I don't think we have a choice."

Pop rubbed his hands together. "I'll wait for the forensics team then I'll get her on back to the morgue. She sure can't stay here all night."

Actually, she could if Pop deemed it necessary. But Brock didn't expect the man to be that dedicated.

Pop looked around. "Although it's as cold out here as it is in the freezer."

Gisella lifted her hat from her head and settled it back into place. "That'll have to be the plan then. After the forensics team finishes, you get her to the morgue." She sighed. "Brock, do you have your camera?"

"Yeah. Let me get it from the car."

She nodded and told Pop, "Let us get some pictures of her like she is now. We don't want to rely on our memories, that's for sure."

"That's fine. I'm going to go get a body bag and the stretcher. Once you're done with your pictures, I'll load her up."

"Thanks."

Brock returned within minutes, Niles Vernon walking beside him. With a gloved hand, the man held up a cigarette. "Found this in the trees over yonder. I can send this off to the lab in El Paso and see what they can come up with. Seems like a fresh one to me."

Gisella stepped forward and handed the man a bag. He dropped it in and she smiled her thanks. "Good job."

Brock adjusted the camera to shoot in the dark and began snapping. He wanted pictures from every angle. Once the body was moved, they couldn't come back for more.

Finally, he decided he had enough and motioned for Pop to take over.

The sheriff and Pop loaded the body into the bag

and onto the stretcher. The black coroner car had been converted from an old station wagon. It was large enough to hold two bodies in the back, the driver and a passenger in the front.

Once the back gate was closed, Pop promised to put Ina in the freezer to wait for the medical examiner's arrival.

Gisella sidled up to Brock as they watched the man drive off. "I don't like this one bit."

"I'm with you, but we don't have much to work with."

"No, I mean someone seems to be able to keep one step ahead of us. How did the person who killed Ina know we would be here tonight?"

Brock shrugged. "Maybe she trusted the wrong person?"

Gisella planted her hands on her hips. "Maybe."

"You think someone overheard our conversation?"

"I don't know. She called you at the church. Maybe Pastor Ruben wasn't the only person there."

Brock looked doubtful. "Possibly. I still think the most likely scenario is that Ina trusted someone she shouldn't have. Told someone she was going to meet us."

"Krista?"

"Maybe. They seemed to be friends. If Ina did tell Krista in the restaurant, she could have been easily overheard there."

"Let's make a point to ask her." Gisella headed back to the car and Brock followed her. "I hope we got everything back there," she muttered. "I really don't want this guy to get away with her murder."

"I think she put up a pretty good fight. Did you see her fingernails?"

"Yes."

"I wonder where she scratched him." Brock looked thoughtful. "Let's keep our eyes open for anyone with fresh wounds."

"Sounds like a plan to me."

"Now," he yawned as he slid into the driver's seat. "My adrenaline's just crashed. Let's get some rest. I have a feeling tomorrow is going to be a long day."

The next morning, Gisella met Brock in the lobby of the small hotel for surprisingly good bagels and hot coffee. She lifted a brow as he downed three bagels in as many bites. "Hungry?"

"Yeah, I missed my midnight snack last night."

She smiled. "We were kinda busy around midnight."

"Exactly." He grabbed another one, wrapped it in a napkin and said, "Cinnamon raisin. My favorite."

Gisella wrinkled her nose. "I like the plain ones with butter."

Brock shook his head, his expression woefully sad. "No sense of adventure at all, huh?"

"Right," she snorted. "That's why I chose the profession I'm in."

He laughed then sobered. With a nod to Steve, the hotel clerk, he said, "I wonder if he ever stops cleaning?" The man sprayed the counter and wiped.

"Probably picked it up in prison."

"That'll do it."

The family of three entered the dining area and Gisella smiled at the little girl. The tot hid her face behind her mother's skirts and Gisella felt a pang of longing. Would she ever have children?

Oblivious to her inner angst, Brock said, "Come on. Let's head over to the morgue and see if our ME's here yet."

A glance at her watch showed it was almost 8:30. "Sounds good to me." Gisella grabbed her fawn-colored felt hat from the table and pressed it on her head. She didn't need to be thinking about marriage and children right now. She needed to stay focused on doing her job.

A few minutes later, they walked into the small doctor's office. A woman in her early thirties greeted them. "I'm Sophia Hayes, the secretary. Dr. Barnard said to show you on back to where we have the body." Her eyes teared and she sniffed. "I'm sorry. I'm friends with Ina's mother. She's just devastated."

Gisella's heart ached for her pain. "We're going to find who did this to her."

The woman shrugged. "I hope so, but it still won't bring Ina back."

"No. No, it won't." They walked down a small hallway that connected to a locked door. Ms. Hayes swiped her card and stepped inside a room. The temperature dropped by ten degrees. "She's in there." She pointed to the wall that held three oversized drawers. Only one had a label.

Brock thanked her.

"Sure." She frowned and paused.

"What is it?" Gisella asked.

"Well, you wouldn't be here to claim the body, so if you don't mind me asking…why exactly are you here?"

"We're here to see what the medical examiner finds."

A brow lifted. "Medical examiner?"

Gisella shot a look at Brock. "Yes, he's coming in this morning from El Paso to gather evidence from her to see if there's anything that will help track down who killed her. Didn't the sheriff or Pop explain this when they brought the body in last night?"

"Well, I wasn't here last night and no, no one explained anything. I just found a note on my desk saying you two would be in this morning and to accommodate you as necessary."

"Okay, so there wasn't anything about the ME coming from El Paso?"

"No, nothing."

Brock stepped forward. "It doesn't matter. As long as he can get the evidence we need, the lack of communication isn't an issue."

"Um…I'm afraid it is." Sophia swallowed. "Ina's already been cleaned up and prepared for the autopsy."

"What?" Gisella nearly yelled the word. Taking a deep breath, she blew it out then said, "What do you mean cleaned up? She wasn't supposed to be touched."

The woman paled. "I… I'm sorry. I didn't know. I called Mrs. Delgado, the mortician, who also works as the autopsy team this morning like I always do when we have a death. I told her about Ina and she came right away. She always comes in around 5:30 in the morning before Pop goes in to the restaurant. She stays with Pop's wife during the day because she can't be left alone."

"So, Mrs. Delgado's already come and gone."

"Yes."

Gisella placed a hand on her head and paced from one end of the room to the other. "Great."

Brock rubbed his chin. "Well, there's nothing we can do about it now. Have the ME come on back when he gets here. Maybe she missed something and he'll find it."

Ms. Hayes nodded. "I'm so sorry. I truly didn't know."

Gisella offered her a gentle smile. "It's not your

fault." Pop should have been a bit more clear in his note, she thought.

A buzzer sounded and Ms. Hayes said, "That's the signal someone's come in. I better check and see who that is."

She started out the door when the sheriff appeared in the hall. He entered the room. "Well? The ME get here?"

Brock rubbed his eyes. "No, but it doesn't matter. Doesn't look like we'll be needing his services after all."

"What?" Twin creases appeared in Sheriff Johnston's forehead as he frowned. "What do you mean?"

They explained.

A red flush crept up into his cheeks and his eyes narrowed. "Who gave the order that the body was to be prepared for burial?"

Ms. Hayes shrugged. "No order, Sheriff. You know I always notify Mrs. Delgado if there's a death. I call her or send her a text when we have a body and she comes on over to do her thing."

The sheriff blew out a sigh.

Before he could say anything more, a buzzer sounded. Ms. Hayes jumped. "That's the front door again. I'll get it."

Gisella looked at Brock. "The ME, probably."

"I'll fill him in on everything." Brock left the way they came in.

While she waited for Brock, Gisella examined the room. Small, yet functional. It fit the size of the town.

One thing that caught her attention was the large board that covered one wall of the room. She walked over to it. What was it?

Boot Hill Cemetery in big capital letters graced the top. As she studied it, she realized it was the cemetery blueprint. With small squares containing letters.

Plots? Already in use or ones bought for the future?

The door opened behind her and she turned to see Brock enter with the medical examiner from El Paso. Brock said, "This is Horatio Chavez. I already told him what happened with the body. He said he'd give her a once-over anyway."

Pop lumbered in and moved to the drawer with the label. After pulling on a pair of gloves, he grasped the handle and said, "I'm real sorry about the mix-up. Sometimes communication around here isn't the best." He slid her out.

Ina Jaramillo.

Gisella drew in a deep breath and studied the poor girl.

The ME pulled on his gloves and got to work.

Brock and Gisella watched. Horatio looked up. "I'm going to be a little while. You want to come back in about an hour or so?"

Gisella sighed. "Sure."

As they headed to the door to leave, Horatio called them back. "Hey, where are her clothes? If someone bagged them, I might be able to get something off them."

"I'll ask." Gisella found the receptionist. "I need Ina's clothes. Do you know where they are?"

Sophia frowned. "I think Mrs. Delgado placed them in the cabinet for Ina's mother to pick them up."

Finally, something positive. For a moment, she'd feared the woman was going to say they'd been washed and sent home.

Gisella reentered the morgue and kept her gaze averted from the actions on the steel table. Death didn't bother her much. It was a part of life. Yes, she felt sorry for the victims and the families. Her heart hurt for them, but in her job, she learned to distance herself from it and move on. If she couldn't do that, she couldn't do her job.

However, watching autopsies wasn't at the top of her ten favorite things to do and she avoided them at all costs. She opened the cabinet and found the clothes in a plastic bag. Grabbing it, she placed it on the counter. "Here you go."

Horatio looked up. "Great. I have a feeling that's going to be our best bet."

"Call if you get anything interesting."

"Will do."

They exited the morgue and walked down the street to the police station. Brock nodded toward the sheriff's office.

Sheriff Johnston was walking inside. He stopped when he saw them and motioned for them to join him.

"Wonder what he wants?" Gisella murmured.

"Let's go find out."

Brock and Gisella entered the sheriff's office. Gisella inhaled the smell of strong coffee and air freshener. She almost smiled to herself. A small-town police station didn't smell much different than one in the big city. She looked around. "Where'd the sheriff go?"

Brock shook his head.

After checking in with the lone secretary at the entrance, they were directed to "the third door on the right at the end of the hallway."

They walked single file down the narrow hall. Gisella led the way. She could feel Brock behind her and wondered at her acute perception of his presence.

Entering the room, Gisella found Chris Locke seated behind an old wooden desk. He looked up and frowned. "Can I help you?"

"The sheriff motioned for us to come on in. Do you know where he went?"

Chris grunted and offered, "Sheriff Johnston got a phone call as soon as he stepped in the door. He went to investigate a disturbance. One he always handles. But he wanted me to show y'all this."

He reached across his desk and picked up a plastic bag. A small skull-and-crossbones earring glinted from within. "This belongs to Ina's boyfriend, Clinton Green."

"Where'd you find it?" Brock asked.

"In the cemetery not too far from where Ina was found." He placed the evidence in Brock's outstretched palm. "I went back out there this morning at first light to see if we missed anything." He nodded at the earring. "We did."

"So where's this boyfriend?" Gisella asked as she stepped closer to get a better look at the earring. She noted that Chris's animosity was nowhere to be found during this exchange. She looked at him a little closer and decided that when he wasn't radiating attitude, he could be someone she wouldn't mind working with.

"We're a little short-staffed so Niles volunteered to track Clinton down now. Clinton works at Jacko's Auto Store as a mechanic. Should be back any minute now—assuming Clinton showed up for work after his adventures last night."

"He showed up." Gisella and Brock turned to see Niles standing behind them. A scared young man with a bad haircut stood next to him. Gisella thought he looked a bit like an ostrich looking for the nearest pile of sand.

Brock looked at him. "Were you at the graveyard last night?"

Clinton's scrawny throat moved convulsively as he swallowed several times. "Yes, sir."

"Did you kill Ina?"

ELEVEN

At the mention of Ina's name, Clinton's eyes teared up. "No, sir."

"You know who did?"

He blinked rapidly and shook his head. "No."

Niles gave him a shove into Chris's office and said, "Sit."

Clinton sat.

Gisella eyed him. He looked like a scared kid. "How old are you?"

"Twenty-four."

She reached for the bag that contained the earring. "Is this yours?"

More swallowing. His hand shook as he reached up to finger his bare left ear. "Um…yes, ma'am."

She leaned in. "But you didn't kill her?"

"No. I…I was supposed to meet her there about 8:30, but I got held up at home. I was late. By the time I got there, she was dead."

Gisella looked at him. "She was supposed to meet us at 9:00. Did you know that?"

His eyes went wide. "No, ma'am, I didn't. But that doesn't mean anything. Ina has…had gotten real secretive lately."

"Secretive?"

He bobbed his head.

"How? Secretive of what?"

A shrug. "I don't know, but she just wasn't her usual happy self."

"So what did you do when you found her?"

He shivered. "I ran."

Chris looked at him. "You didn't think you should call for help?"

"N-no. I mean, yes, but… I mean…" He broke off and buried his face in his hands. Silence echoed in the room broken only by the sound of the young man's sobs.

When he finally had himself under control, Gisella shifted and said, "Look, Mr. Green, like I said, Ina was supposed to meet us last night at 9:00 to share some information with us. Do you know of anything she knew that someone wouldn't want her telling us?"

He shook his head. "She never said nothing. But…"

"What?"

"She was acting funny. Scared."

Niles crossed his arms across his burly chest. "Scared of what?"

"She wouldn't tell me. She just acted paranoid

every time we were out. She got to the point where she didn't want to go out at night at all. She'd only go to work, but if I dropped in on her to say hey, she was always looking around to see who was listening." He shrugged. "Stuff like that. I don't know."

Gisella asked, "Do you know anything about the Lions of Texas?"

"Who?"

The blank look on his face answered her question.

Brock shifted his arms across his chest and asked, "Do you own a gun?"

"Sure. Everyone around here owns a gun. This close to the border, you'd be crazy not to own one."

"What kind of gun is it?" Gisella asked. She wanted to be able to compare it to ballistics on the bullet casings they'd found around the scene.

"I got a rifle and a .357 Magnum."

She looked at Brock. "We get any feedback on the casings?"

He shook his head. "Not yet."

Chris cocked his head at Clinton. "You fire that gun recently?"

"No, sir, I sure haven't."

Niles motioned for the man to stand. "Well, come on, I'll follow you home and you can show me the guns." He narrowed his eyes. "And I'll be able to tell if you're lying."

"I'm not lying."

Clinton stood and Gisella sighed as she looked at Vernon. "Is there any proof other than the earring that he had anything to do with her death?"

"Nope. And I can confirm his alibi when I go check the guns."

Clinton nodded and began to gnaw on an already decimated fingernail. But he didn't look scared anymore, just…like he was grieving.

Gisella thought of one more question. "Do you have any fresh scratches on you?"

He frowned at her. "Fresh scratches? No, why?"

Gisella pictured the skin and dirt under Ina's fingernails. "Just wondering." The woman would have gone for the face or whatever exposed skin was within scratching distance. She nodded to Clinton's hands. "Can you push up your sleeves and hold your hands out?"

He did so.

Pale skin stared back at her. Clear, unblemished skin. "Okay, thanks."

Clinton pulled his sleeves back down and Niles clapped him on the shoulder. "Let's go." He pointed him to the door. Looking like he might burst into tears, the young man slouched out as though ashamed of his crane-like height.

Compassion crimping her heart, Gisella stopped him with a hand on his arm. "I'm so sorry for your loss," she said softly.

He nodded, gratitude appearing in his eyes. Without another word, he left, followed closely by Niles Vernon.

Once they were gone, Gisella looked at the two remaining men. "I think I'm going to head back over to the morgue to see what our ME came up with. Will you let us know what the sheriff finds out?"

Chris shrugged. "Sure."

Brock followed her from the office. "What do you think?"

"I think something very strange is going on in this town. And I don't think Clinton has a clue. I do, however, think he was in love with Ina and is heartbroken at her death."

"So you don't think he's our guy?"

"Nope. Do you?"

"No."

She smiled up at him. "Glad to know we're on the same page."

As they stepped back outside and headed for the morgue, Brock looked around. "You know, everything seems normal. Life is going on around us. But, the people…I don't think they're so much unfriendly as they are…"

"…scared?" She finished for him.

He cocked a brow at her. "So, you've noticed that, too?"

"I have." She glanced up the street one way, then back down the other. And shivered. "And every time we're out in the open, do you feel…exposed? Like you have a big bull's-eye on your forehead?"

"Yes. And I don't like it." He took her arm and this time her shiver had nothing to do with feeling like eyes followed her every move. It had to do with being next to him, near him. Breathing in his unique scent—and liking it very much.

As subtly as possible, she pulled away from his grasp and picked up the pace.

They arrived back at the morgue within minutes and this time the secretary led them to the back without question.

They found Chavez bent over Ina putting stitches in the Y incision. He looked up when they entered. "I'm just about finished."

"Did you find anything?" Gisella asked as she moved closer.

A sigh filtered from the man's lips. "Not really. She was cleaned up pretty good. All of her internal organs were normal. She was killed due to asphyxiation like the bruises on her neck indicated."

"So definitely strangled," Brock muttered.

"Yep. And I did manage to get some possible tissue from under a couple of nails. Other than that…"

"We'll take what we can get," Gisella said. She watched Pop—who'd assisted Chavez with the autopsy—remove his gloves, wash his hands, then grab a pen.

He walked over to the big map of the cemetery Gisella had studied earlier. He stood in front of it, ran his finger along some of the boxes, then filled in an empty one.

She looked closer to see what he'd written. IJ. "Is that where she's to be buried?" she asked.

Pop nodded. "Yes."

Brock stood behind her, looking, too. Once again, she felt his presence in a way that bothered her. Big time. Goose bumps pebbled up on her arms and she blinked. Clearing her throat, she caught her breath as she noted, "It's not too far from where she was killed. How sad."

"No kidding," Brock said. He sighed and straightened. "What do you say we—"

Gisella's phone interrupted whatever he was going to say. Snatching it from the clip on her side, she pressed the Talk button. "Hello?"

"Hey, Gisella, this is Anderson."

Anderson Michaels, another Ranger determined to get to the bottom—or the top—of the Lions of Texas. "What's going on, Anderson?"

"Our guy in the coma woke up."

"No kidding." Excitement thrummed through Gisella. "Did he say who shot him?"

The room went still and she noticed she had everyone's attention.

"Not yet," Anderson said. "He's only opened his

eyes a few times, but it turns out that Quin Morton is a former Real Irish Republican Army member."

Shocked, Gisella went silent as she processed what that might mean. "What? A terrorist? What's he doing with the Lions?"

"A good question." Anderson's sigh filtered through the line. "And one we're working on figuring out."

"How did you figure out he was a terrorist?"

"Interpol came through for us. The guy's kept a low profile for the most part, but they finally managed to track him when one of their undercover agents thought she recognized him. From there, it was only a matter of time."

Gisella eyed Brock. His furrowed brow told her he was listening to the conversation with intent curiosity. She didn't mind; she'd have to fill him in anyway.

Anderson continued his report. "Mr. Morton is still under 24/7 guard as we don't want to take a chance on any more attempts on his life. Someone didn't want him to wake up."

"Can he communicate at all?"

"He can blink. He's been answering some yes-or-no questions, but apparently no one is asking the right questions because every time he's questioned he gets very agitated and his heart rate speeds up."

"Ouch." She winced.

"Yes. So we've been officially banned from his room until he recovers more."

"Great."

"Tell me about it." His disgust with the situation came through loud and clear.

Gisella said, "All right, thank for the update. Let me know if anything else develops."

"Will do. Stay out of trouble, Hernandez."

She gave a short laugh. "Will do, Michaels." Hanging up the phone she shook her head. While she didn't doubt she'd earned the respect of her fellow male Rangers, every once in a while one of them would slip up and treat her like a kid sister. From them she didn't mind it so much. But if anyone else—like Brock—tried that, she'd have his head.

Chavez snapped his gloves off and headed for the sink. "I'll do my best to put a rush on this. No guarantees on the timeline."

Brock nodded his thanks and pointed to the door. To Gisella, he said, "Come on, let's get something to eat. I'm starving. You can fill me in on the way."

Brock reached around her to pull open the heavy glass door.

As Gisella stepped past him, her shoulder brushed his chest. His hand came up to rest on her lower back as though to help escort her down the short set of stairs. Heart thumping double time at his touch, she pulled away and looked at him, confusion racing. "I can…"

The wood above the door exploded, raining bits and pieces down on them.

TWELVE

Brock shoved Gisella behind the bushes beside the porch and dove right after her. Landing with a grunt, he heard the screams of the people on the street and prayed they'd taken cover.

Gisella rolled away and gasped, "We've got to find better cover than these bushes."

"Go that way." He pointed toward a cement wall about five bushes down. Oh, God. I guess I'm praying again. *Keep us safe, please.*

As Gisella crawled another shot sounded and the bush in front of her shuddered as the bullet pierced the middle and buried itself into the cement behind. Fragments exploded from the building. Gisella flinched but kept moving.

Gritting his teeth, Brock stayed right behind her. She sprawled flat on the ground. He grabbed the back of her shirt and yanked her up. He kept his eye on the cement wall expecting to feel a bullet slam into him at any moment.

Or watch one slam into her.

What seemed to stretch into ten minutes really only lasted for less than ten seconds.

Brock followed as Gisella threw herself behind the protection of the wall just as a bullet pinged into the building above them.

A siren sounded in the distance.

Panting, her gun in her hand, Gisella peered around the edge of the wall.

"What do you see?" His voice sounded raspy to his own ears. His heart thudded in his throat and he realized he wasn't nearly as worried about a bullet finding him as he was about Gisella getting hurt.

A new kind of fear settled in his chest.

But he couldn't worry about that now.

Gisella's shoulders tensed. "I see someone on top of that grocery store. If you look at where the bullets are hitting, it makes sense."

Brock had his phone out. The siren screamed louder. "Sheriff's on his way, I bet."

"Our shooter's not getting away if I have anything to say about it."

"What are you planning?" Brock shifted behind her. He'd already dialed the sheriff's number, but the man wasn't picking up. Probably on the line with someone else.

She never took her eyes from the building in front of her. "He's got to come down. Where would you go from there?"

"I'd have a car waiting. Or at least a good escape

route planned that would be easy to navigate on foot and lose anyone chasing me."

Gisella finally looked back at him. "You want to go right while I go left?"

His slight hesitation made her frown and he told himself to get over it. She could handle herself.

And save his life while she was at it, she would no doubt remind him.

Nodding, he motioned for her to go. She did. He followed then branched off to the right. No gunshots sounded.

He made it to the back of the building and found the steps that led to the roof. Brock stopped and dialed the sheriff's number.

Johnston answered on the first ring and barked, "What's going on in my town, Martin?"

"We need to evacuate the grocery store on Main. Get everyone off the street and…"

"Where's the shooter?"

"I'm going after him." *As soon as I can find him.* Brock didn't see Gisella. Where was she?

No sooner had he thought the question than he saw her dart after a fleeing figure. The masked man dodged a parked car, heading for the end of the building.

"Freeze!" Gisella shouted. The man ignored her. Gisella noted as many details about him as she could. He was taller than her, thin and light on his feet.

Brock spun on his heel and yanked at the back

door to the store. Locked. Running out of time, he sped across the lot in the opposite direction Gisella had taken. He took a quick right, which brought him to the front of the store.

Just in time to see Gisella and the man coming his way. Fortunately, the front of the building was deserted. He figured the front door was probably locked, too. He gave it a tug to make sure. Relief filled him. The people inside were safe for now.

Gripping his weapon, Brock dove behind a parked vehicle and watched from underneath. An idea hit him. He wanted this guy alive and thought he might know how to go about catching him and keeping him that way.

Sliding under the truck that had been jacked up on four oversize tires, Brock lay on his back, head turned, watching, his gun ready just in case the guy decided to turn and try to get off a shot at Gisella.

Fortunately, he seemed more intent on getting away than shooting anymore. And hopefully, he was looking up and not down. Brock saw the man's hands were empty. But that didn't mean he didn't have a weapon on him.

Scooting closer to the edge, Brock waited.

Almost.

Now.

Brock swung a leg out from under the truck, catching the fleeing suspect in the shins.

A surprised yell escaped the man before being cut

short when he slammed onto the asphalt. Another cry of pain ripped from him even as he desperately tried to keep going, crab-style. Lightning-quick, Gisella was on him while Brock scrambled from beneath the truck.

"Freeze!" she shouted again as she landed with a knee in the suspect's back, forcing him back down. He screamed in pain, either from Gisella's knee or the scrapes and cuts he had from head-butting the ground.

Brock made it to his feet, his eyes scanning for a weapon. Seeing none, he stepped on the suspect's left forearm while Gisella wrestled his right wrist into one of the cuffs. Brock started patting him down while Gisella gritted, "Be still! You're just making this harder on yourself than it has to be."

"Let me go! You've got no right to do this!"

Gisella's lips were so tight they looked almost white. "Brock, take a look at this."

He looked where she pointed.

Three straight scratches on the man's forearm that looked pretty new. He raised his brow at her and said, "I think we've found Ina's killer."

"I think you're right. The question is, who is he?"

She flipped the man over and, for the first time, they got a good look at his face. "Hey, I know you," she sputtered.

She glanced at Brock as they each grabbed an arm and pulled the man to his feet. Blood dripped from some nasty-looking cuts on his face. Gisella narrowed her eyes and said, "You're the snarky one who stormed from the diner and told me to figure out for myself who you were."

He offered her a sneer.

She glared. "Well, Jasper West, why were you shooting at us?"

When she said his name, he jerked as though she'd slapped him. Then glared back. But kept his mouth shut.

By this time, the sheriff had arrived with two of his deputies. Leaving his lights flashing a red warning, he hauled himself out of the vehicle. Chris Locke and Niles Vernon pulled in three seconds later.

Sheriff Johnston shoved his hat back on his head and took in the scene with a glint in his narrowed eyes. Looking at Gisella, he placed his hands on his hips. "I'm not sure what to think about all the trouble that's showing up in my town so soon after your arrival."

Brock simply looked at the man. "Looks like we're making a few people nervous."

A short laugh escaped the sheriff. "I'd say. What happened?"

Brock filled him in.

Turning his attention to Jasper, the sheriff shook his head. "We've suspected Jasper of smuggling drugs across the border. Niles has been watching him for a while now. Let's give him the pleasure of questioning our prisoner." He scratched his chin.

The Border Patrol agent smirked at Jasper. "I told you I'd get you one way or another. This little stunt will earn us a search warrant, which will prove what I've suspected all along."

"Hey!" Jasper protested. "I don't smuggle drugs."

Gisella snorted. "No, you just try to kill cops. That's *so* much better."

Jasper snarled in her direction and yelled a few choice words, which she tuned out.

"Guess we better get him cleaned up and down to the office for some questioning." Niles gave a glance around. "Where's the weapon?"

"Missing," Gisella offered. "But as soon as we trace his steps, we'll come across it. I just hope we find it before some kid gets a hold of it. Have his hands and clothing tested for gunpowder residue."

Furrowing his brow, the sheriff jutted a jaw at Chris. "See if you can find it."

Chris nodded and Gisella held up a hand to stop him. "He was on top of the grocery store when he took the shots. You might start there and work your way down."

"Got it." The deputy took off and Brock shoved the now quiet, but still clearly defiant prisoner toward the sheriff's car.

"I guess he belongs to you now. I'd like to see if his prints match any of the ones found in Gisella's hotel room. Get him downtown and we'll be by soon to question him."

A flicker of something crossed Jasper's face and Gisella figured Brock was on to something. Brock must have noticed it, too, because he leaned in and asked, "Bought any red spray paint lately?"

Jasper's lip curled and he looked like he wanted to spit in Brock's eye. Instead of giving him the opportunity, Brock pulled back and slammed the door. "Good riddance."

Gisella sidled up to Brock as Sheriff Johnston drove Jasper the short distance to the jail located behind the sheriff's office. "Heard anything from your friend in the lab?"

He looked at his phone. "Nope. She'll call when she has something ready for me."

Gisella cut her eyes at him. "I knew it was a 'she.'"

Questioning Jasper West was the top priority. If he had information that could lead them to the Lions of Texas's head honcho, Gisella wanted it. Now.

She strode into the office the sheriff used as an interrogation room and looked at Jasper. He sat at the table head tilted listening to the man on his left.

Brock stood behind her.

The sheriff sat at the table opposite the lawyer and his client filling out paperwork.

Jasper already had a lawyer. Brock raised a brow and looked at Gisella. "That was fast."

Sheriff Johnston looked up from his papers. "I let him call from the car." He gave a shrug. "I figured the faster he got here, the faster we could get everything done. Simon Holmes, Boot Hill's busiest lawyer."

Simon Holmes lifted his brow. "I'm the only lawyer."

Gisella sat next to the sheriff, noting that Mr. Holmes looked to be in his early sixties with gray hair and sharp green eyes.

Brock stepped farther into the room and took up residence against the wall. He crossed his arms across his chest. "Do you mind if we ask a few questions?"

The lawyer looked at him. "Go ahead. I'll direct him as to whether or not he should answer."

Brock looked at the man who'd shot at them. "Who told you to kill us?"

Without waiting for his lawyer's input, Jasper gave a snort. "If I'd been told to kill you, you'd be dead."

"Jasper…" the lawyer muttered under his breath.

Gisella tapped her lips and gave him a thoughtful look. "You weren't working on your own. You had orders." Her soft voice brought them all to attention. "Someone doesn't like the questions we're asking. You can sit there and deny it all you want, but we're making someone nervous. I know you don't care about helping us out, but do you really want to take the fall for this all alone?"

Jasper licked his lips and his gaze darted, bouncing off everyone in the room before landing on the table in front of him. Then he gave a small smile. "You're right. I don't want to take the fall. And I won't. I got friends. I'll get out of this because I didn't do anything."

"Jasper, that's enough." Mr. Holmes clasped his hands in front of him.

A knock on the door swung their attention to Chris Locke who joined them—with a rifle in his gloved right hand.

Gisella sat up straight. "Is that the weapon?"

Chris nodded. "I'm willing to bet it is. Ballistics will have to confirm it. I found it in a Dumpster out behind the back of the grocery store." He sniffed it. "Recently fired. I'm getting ready to send it to the lab in El Paso. Just have to wrap it up and ship it off."

Jasper simply looked at them. Gisella frowned. He didn't appear to be worried about the fact that they had the rifle. "Jasper, are we going to find your prints on this weapon?"

He smirked. "I doubt it."

Gisella huffed a disgusted sigh. "One more question. Did you kill Ina?"

"Ina who?" The tip of his tongue circled his lips then he made a popping sound. It was all Gisella could do to contain herself. She wanted to launch across the table, grasp his neck and demand he tell her what she wanted to know.

Instead, she stood and looked at the sheriff. "I'm not wasting any more time on him."

The sheriff grunted, stood and pulled Jasper to his feet. "Come on. Maybe some time in your cell all alone with your thoughts will make you feel like talking."

The sheriff led Jasper away and Gisella dropped her head in her hands.

Once they were alone, Brock asked, "Are you all right?"

She looked up. "I'm fine. Just trying to figure out the next step."

"Let's go over what we know."

"We know drugs are coming in over the border into Boot Hill."

"And someone in this town knows something."

Gisella pursed her lips. "Ina knew something."

"But her boyfriend didn't."

She cocked her head. "What about her family?"

He nodded. "I think that might be the next step. At least until we can get Mr. West to cooperate and tell us what he knows."

Gisella tapped the table with her hand. "And that's another thing. Did you notice that Jasper didn't seem too concerned about being caught?"

"I did. I want to dig a little deeper into his background and see who his friends are."

Together they rose and Gisella pulled out her phone to call her boss. Ben answered on the second ring.

"What do you have for me, Gisella?"

"A lot of puzzle pieces, but none that seem to fit together very well." She filled him on the latest.

"What do you need from me?"

"I need some background on Jasper West. I want to know what his connections are."

"All right. I'll have someone get right on that and get back to you."

She thanked him. "How is Quin Morton? Is he talking yet? Any progress there?"

A sigh filtered to her. "Not really. The doctors still won't let us in to question him like we need to."

Frustration ate at her. This whole case could be blown wide open if the man with the answers would wake up and talk.

But until that happened, she had to keep digging, keep after the answers and find them some other way. "All right, Ben. I'll let you know if anything else turns up."

She hung up and looked at Brock. "You want to question Ina's friends and family?"

"Let's go."

As they exited the building, he placed a hand at the small of her back and this time the ripples of awareness that shivered up her spine didn't surprise her. From the corner of her eye, she looked at the man beside her. In a different time, a different place…he would have been a definite possibility.

THIRTEEN

Ina's home sat on about an acre of land on the outskirts of the small town. The double-wide trailer with its trimmed hedges and overflowing flower pots said someone took care of it even though money was in short supply.

A pickup truck sat in the yard and a pitbull stood to attention when they pulled up in front.

"Can we get past the dog to knock on the door?" Brock muttered.

"I think he's tied to that tree."

"You think? Let's make sure."

She eyed him with amusement. "Are you scared of dogs?"

He glared at her even while he felt the flush of embarrassment start to creep up the back of his neck. "Just the ones that bite."

The amusement faded. "When did you get bitten?"

"When I was six."

She patted his hand and his embarrassment started

to recede. Now why had he shared that with her? He kept his fear of big dogs locked away in the recesses of his mind and never brought out the key.

Only in a few short minutes, she had him blurting it out. He looked at her a little closer. What was it about this woman that made him want to be open? Vulnerable? Why did he find himself wanting her to know everything about him?

Scary. And yet thrilling at the same time. He'd never felt this way before and he wanted the opportunity to explore the feelings. See where it could lead.

But what would she say about that?

Gisella pulled her hand away and he missed the contact. When she opened her door, the dog lunged to the end of the chain and Brock reached out to yank her back inside the vehicle. "Don't."

She shook him off. "He's fine. I'll be fine. He's not even barking. I think he just wants some company." Giving him one last look, she got out and slammed her door shut.

With a resigned sigh, Brock opened his door and climbed out, too. He couldn't let her go by herself. Eyeing the dog, Brock finally noticed the chain was taut. And as she said, the dog wasn't barking. Just keeping a close watch on those invading his territory.

Gisella spoke softly to the animal and finally its

hind end started wagging. Walking past the now-docile dog, she reached the porch and climbed the steps to knock on the door. Brock followed her.

Shuffling footsteps sounded from inside and within seconds, someone called out in Spanish, "*¿Quién está?* Who is it?"

Responding in the same language, Gisella told her.

The door opened and a woman in her midfifties stared up at them from red-rimmed eyes. "What do you want?"

Brock flashed his badge then offered, also in Spanish, "We're sorry about your loss, but would you mind if we talked to you a little bit about Ina? We're trying to find out who killed her."

The door opened wider and the woman stepped back. "I'm Ina's mother, Honoria. Come in."

She led them to a worn but clean couch and motioned for them to sit. Brock noticed a Bible on the end table and an ornate cross hanging on the wall above the couch.

Gisella sat and asked, "Do you live here alone?"

Honoria nodded her head as she took a seat in the rocker next to her. "Yes. My other daughter, Francesca, lives in El Paso. Ina…" She trailed off and swallowed hard. "I don't know what I will do without her," she finally whispered.

Pain flashed across Gisella's face and she leaned

forward to cover the woman's hand. "You have a cross on your wall. Do you believe what that stands for?"

"*Sí.*" Her lips trembled.

"Then let Him be your strength."

The woman nodded. "*Sí,* I will have to." She gave a sad shrug. "There is no other choice."

Brock felt his heart do that weird trembling thing it seemed to do whenever he witnessed Gisella's sincere compassion, her reaching out to those in need who had been hurt by life. He realized that not only did he want to open himself up to Gisella and let her know everything about him, he wanted her to reciprocate. To let him into her deepest thoughts and to know her completely. He swallowed hard and focused on what she was saying.

"Señora Jaramillo, we talked with Ina's boyfriend, Clinton, and while he was at the graveyard the night she was killed, we don't believe he had anything to do with it."

"No." Señora Jaramillo shook her head. "He would not hurt a hair on her head. He loved that girl and wanted to marry her."

"We think so, too, but we also think that Ina was somehow involved in the drugs coming over from Juarez. Do you know anything?"

The woman's eyes flickered, pain crossed her face and she bowed her head.

"Señora?" Gisella leaned forward.

"I do not know for sure. I just know she had more money than she should have. I didn't ask where it came from and she didn't tell me."

Brock rested his forearms on his thighs as he shifted to say, "Ina was supposed to meet us the night she was killed. We think someone found out and decided to make sure she didn't talk to us."

A wail of grief exploded from the woman's throat and Brock flinched. Gisella's eyes teared up and he watched her quickly hide them.

"Señora…" Gisella's words trailed off.

After a few minutes of uncontrollable crying, Señora Jaramillo gathered herself together. "I'm sorry," she whispered. "I just worked so hard to make sure my children stayed away from that kind of stuff. Those kind of people. And for you to say…" She shook her head and swiped her tears. "I convinced myself that she got the money working in the diner. Or that Clinton gave it to her, but deep down…" She patted her chest. "I wondered."

"Can you think of anyone she may have mentioned that you thought was strange? Any place she was seen that she shouldn't have been?"

"No. No." Señora Jamarillo got up to pace.

"Can we search her room?" Gisella asked.

That stopped her. She seemed to consider it, then with slumped shoulders, gave a slow nod. "*Sí*, first door on the right, down the hall. If you find drugs, I do not want to know, okay?"

Brock exchanged a look with Gisella. "Let's just see if we find anything first."

FOURTEEN

Gisella stopped at the entrance to Ina's room and looked around. Brock came up behind her and placed his hands on her shoulders. "Are you going to let me in?"

She shivered at his touch and moved aside to let him brush by her. Concentrating on the room, she noticed Ina's favorite color had to be purple. The room was very simple, yet neat and clean.

Gisella wandered over to the dresser and examined the items placed just so. A hairbrush, lipstick and other makeup accessories were placed in a small silver tray. Several framed pictures of family. One of Ina with her arms around her mother, head thrown back and laughing. She didn't look so plain in the pictures. But one photo really caught her attention.

"Hey, Brock," she called. "Look at this."

He'd been in the closet. Sticking his head out, he lifted a brow at her. She waved the photo at him. "You recognize anyone in this?"

Fully exiting, he came to stand beside her. She

handed him the picture. "Isn't that the little waitress from the diner? Krista?"

"That's her."

"So she and Ina look to be pretty big buddies. More so than just coworkers." Ina had Krista on her back piggyback-style. The two were waving at the camera, laughing. "I think our first instincts were right. We need to question her and find out what she knows."

"She definitely moved up on the priority list."

They took the photo back into the living area where Señora Jaramillo sat in her rocker staring into space. At their appearance, she blinked. Gisella showed her the picture.

"What is this girl, Krista, to Ina?"

The woman took the picture and studied it. "Ina used to babysit her when Krista was younger. Ina became like a big sister to Krista who has no brothers or sisters. Now they're just friends. Or...they were." More tears appeared and Señora Jaramillo managed to swallow them before they fell.

Gisella smiled. "Thank you. I think we're done now. And again, we're very sorry about Ina." Gisella felt slightly guilty. That she and Brock were somehow responsible for the girl's death.

But Ina had called them.

The guilt remained. Was it possible that Gisella and Brock should have insisted that they meet right away?

Then again, Ina might have run and...

It was no use playing "what if". She couldn't change what happened. But she could find Ina's killer. She had a feeling the killer and the Lions were all connected somehow, she just had to find the link.

Stepping back outside, the hairs on her neck lifted once again. She sure was getting that feeling a lot around this little town. Gisella decided she should be used to it by now. Glancing around, she probed the area.

Was someone watching?

Waiting to shoot? Or just wondering what she and Brock were up to?

"Come on, let's get in the car." Brock placed a hand on her arm and hurried her to the vehicle. So, he felt it, too.

Goose bumps danced up and down her arms, but she wasn't sure if it was from Brock's touch or her uneasy feeling that they had bull's-eyes on their foreheads.

Once inside the passenger side of the car, she studied the trailer then said, "Drive off then circle around and come back, will you?"

He nodded and the fact that he didn't question her made her wonder if he'd been thinking the same thing. He pulled out of the yard and drove down the little road that led back to town.

They didn't pass a single car.

When he found a pretty open spot in the road,

he did a three-point turn and headed back to the Jaramillo trailer.

"I felt like someone was watching us when we stepped outside. You felt it, too?" Giselle asked.

Brock nodded. "Yes. But I couldn't pinpoint anyone anywhere."

"Neither could I. I'm a little worried that some-one's been watching Ina's mother thinking she knows something and that she'll talk."

The trailer came back into view and Brock slowed to a crawl and finally a stop behind a copse of trees that probably didn't do a very good job of hiding their car if someone was looking for it.

But might be good enough if no one expected it to be there.

Ten minutes later, when she saw another car pull into the yard next to the pickup truck, Gisella's heart thudded. "You see who that is?"

"Chris Locke and Niles Vernon."

"Wonder what they're doing here?"

A disappointed sigh slipped from Brock. "Prob-ably the same thing we were. Following up on Ina's murder. And while I have to admit, I'm not crazy about Chris's snarly attitude, he still seems like a competent deputy."

Gisella chewed her lip. "That was my take on him, too." She gave a small pout. "I really expected someone else to show up."

"Like who?"

"Whoever was watching us while we were inside."

"You think they're still there?"

She shrugged. "Who knows?"

"That doesn't mean he did it."

"I don't like walking around feeling like I have a big red target on my forehead," he muttered.

She breathed a laugh. "I know." Then she rolled her head to loosen the tight muscles.

Brock watched her for a moment. "Tense?"

"You think? I need a good swim. I don't care what time we get back tonight, I'm making use of that pool." She cut him a glance from the corner of her eye. "And I'm giving you a heads-up where I'll be so you don't have to worry about me. All right?"

His phone rang and he snatched it. "Brock Martin." A pause. "Oh, hey, Steph. Yeah. What do you have?"

He listened for a moment then said, "Thanks a bunch, I owe you big-time."

Brock hung up and sat there staring out the window.

She nudged him with her elbow. "Well?"

"That was the lab. The fingerprint on the spray can matches Jasper West's."

"Yes," she hissed. "Finally, something concrete. He's got to tell us what he knows."

"Let's let him stew overnight in jail and go see him in the morning."

"Sounds good to me. Maybe it'll loosen his

tongue. But I'm going to check in with the sheriff just to make sure he hasn't said anything more."

Gisella dialed the number. Sheriff Johnston answered on the second ring as Brock maneuvered the car back onto the road to head toward town.

"Sheriff Johnston here."

"Hi, Sheriff, this is Ranger Hernandez. I'm just checking in to see if Jasper West has had anything to say since cooling his heels in the jail."

A disgusted sigh came through the line. "Not a word."

Gisella decided to test the waters. "Does he still seem overly confident? Like he's not a bit worried about having consequences for his actions?"

The sheriff snorted. "Yeah, but that's Jasper. His daddy has the biggest spread with the most cattle just outside of town. Jasper hasn't worried much about consequences from the day he was born." A pause. "Although I have to say, this time, Jasper's surprised me. I wouldn't have expected him to try to shoot you in the middle of town. That just shouts stupidity if you ask me."

Gisella agreed. "All right. One more thing. We just spoke with Ina's mother and she had no clue what her daughter was up to. We think someone may have been watching the home and saw us drive up. Will you have someone cruise by the trailer every once in a while just to make sure she's all right? She truly didn't know anything and I'd hate for someone to think she told us something."

"Really? She didn't tell you anything?" Skepticism sounded.

"Nothing. If Ina was involved with something she shouldn't have been—and I believe she was—she kept it from her family."

"Okay, sure. I'll have Locke or one of my other deputies keep an eye on her." A pause. "Who do you think might have been watching the trailer?"

"When I know that, you'll know. Also, one of the prints on the spray can came back belonging to Jasper."

The sheriff grunted. "No kidding. Didn't bother using gloves, huh? What an idiot. I'll question him again with this evidence and see if he has anything he wants to say now."

They disconnected and Gisella filled Brock in. "So I guess that means—"

Her phone vibrated and she glanced at the number. The bottom dropped out of her stomach.

Her dad. She let it go to voice mail. He only called to remind her of all that he and her mother had lost and to beg her to quit her job.

She wasn't getting into that in front of Brock.

"You going to answer that?"

"Nope." Tucking the phone back into her clip on the side of her pants, she ignored his questioning glance when he parked in front of the restaurant.

He let her avoid telling him who she didn't want to talk to. "Want to see what Krista has to say about Ina's murder?"

"If she's here."

Together, they entered the restaurant and Gisella spotted the young girl immediately. Gisella waved her over and could tell she'd been crying.

Krista walked toward them, her shoulders slumped. Gisella felt sorry for the girl. "Hi, Krista."

"Hi." Her red-rimmed eyes were cool, almost hostile. "Just have a seat and I'll be with you in a minute."

"Can we talk?" Gisella asked softly, not holding the girl's frigid reception against her. She probably blamed Gisella and Brock for Ina's death.

"About what?"

"Ina."

Krista's eyes darted around the restaurant. "I don't think so."

Gisella smiled at Brock. "I feel like some dessert. How about you?"

"Sounds good to me."

Krista sighed and pointed to a booth. "Have a seat. I'll be there in a minute."

Gisella and Brock walked to the booth and slid in. Gisella sighed. "She's scared to talk to us."

"Yes, I noticed that."

Picking up the menu, she studied the desserts. "Want to split something?"

"As long as it contains chocolate, I'm good."

Krista approached and stood at the table. "What can I get you?"

"How about the hot fudge brownie with vanilla ice cream?" Gisella figured that would be enough chocolate for the both of them.

"Sure."

Krista started to turn away when Gisella said, "We're sorry about Ina."

The girl sighed and muttered, "She should have been more careful. I shouldn't have helped. I should have just torn up your card and walked away."

Brock leaned forward. "She said she wanted to show us something. Do you know what that might be?"

"No, and I don't want to know." Her gaze flicked to the corner of the restaurant then back and Gisella caught the tears in her eyes just before she whirled from the table and headed for the kitchen.

She watched the girl disappear then felt the hair on the back of her neck rise. When she looked across the restaurant her gaze collided with a pair of watchful, hard brown eyes.

Chris Locke.

He sat alone in his booth drinking from a coffee cup. Lifting it, he offered her a half salute before taking another sip. Gisella nodded back.

As though he'd just made up his mind about something, he set the cup on the table and stood. Then his gaze darted past her and he frowned.

In one smooth move, the deputy placed some bills on the table and headed for the door without breaking stride. The sheriff had just entered and Chris said something to him before exiting. The sheriff's brows knit as he waved in their direction then turned and followed after Chris.

She looked at Brock. "Now that was really weird. Wonder what that was all about?"

"I don't know." He rubbed his chin.

"It's almost like Chris was going to come over and say something, but when the sheriff came in, he changed his mind."

Krista returned with their dessert and two spoons. She placed it in the middle of the table then turned on her heel without a word or a smile.

Brock muttered, "I guess she's not too worried about a tip tonight."

Gisella sighed and picked up one of the spoons. "She's hurting, and I don't think she knows any more than she's told us." Tilting her head, she studied the dessert. "I have to admit I didn't really want this until she put it there."

A mountainous chocolate brownie covered in vanilla ice cream towered between them. Brock never took his eyes from it as he snatched the other spoon and dug in. Gisella wanted to giggle at the sheer delight displayed on his face at the first bite. "It's that good?"

"Definitely. Here." He spooned some more and held it out to her. "Try it."

She laughed. "I have a spoon."

"Trust me. You don't want to wait that long." He pushed the morsel toward her and she opened her lips to take the sugary confection into her mouth. Chocolate and sweet vanilla melted on her tongue. But it was the smoky look in his eyes that had her swallowing. Hard. "Wow."

"Yeah," he whispered. "Wow. You are so beautiful."

Gisella felt her heart stutter. She blinked and gave a shaky laugh. "Um, thanks."

"Seriously. You have a goodness in you that shows from the inside out. How do you keep that from getting snuffed out with the kind of job that you do?"

His question made her stop and think. "I don't know, Brock. I guess I just keep my relationship with the Lord where it needs to be. Even though I have ups and downs like everyone else, I know I'm doing what He wants me to do with my life and I kind of figure as long as I'm doing that, He's going to take care of the rest. You know?"

"I envy that."

Cocking her head, she looked at him. "Why? Aren't you doing what you're supposed to be doing?"

He blew out a sigh. "Sometimes I wonder, but

yeah, most days I believe that I am. And I prayed today for the first time in a long time. It felt good. And right."

She still noticed reservation in his voice. "Then what's the problem?"

"Just all the junk we have to put up with." He kept his voice low. Another bite disappeared before he continued. "Then there's the feeling of being unappreciated. And the feeling that for every bad guy we put away, two more step up to take his place."

Gisella nodded and dipped her spoon for another bite. "I know what you mean, but I can't think about it that way. I think about the fact that when I arrest a drug dealer, I'm saving someone's child, someone's brother or sister." She looked at him, deep into his eyes. "We make a difference, Brock. You have to believe that." Pulling in a deep breath, she sat back and set her spoon down. "At least I have to."

His hand reached out to cover hers and his touch sent shivers all over her once more. Giving her fingers a squeeze, he said, "I'm finished whining." He wiped his mouth with his napkin. "Now, come on, I want to get back to the hotel and check on something."

Gisella stood and pulled out her money. She left a five-dollar bill on the table. "Check on what?"

"I requested a background check on Chris Locke. I asked for it to be emailed to me." He held up his phone. "I just got it, but don't want to read it on here.

It's much easier on the laptop. I thought we could go back to the room and see what Mr. Locke and his surly attitude have been up to."

She grunted. "This whole town feels like one big surly attitude."

He agreed and she led the way to the car thinking about the moment back in the restaurant where he'd shared his dessert with her. With a quiver in her belly, she decided Brock could probably be an incredibly romantic guy.

She wondered if she'd get the chance to be the recipient of that romance.

And realized she wanted to be.

In a really bad way.

Please, Lord, protect not just my physical well-being, but my emotional well-being, too. Cover my heart. Help us solve this case and put it behind us.

Within minutes, they were pulling into the parking lot and Gisella had to push aside her emotions and focus on what needed to be done. From the vehicle window, she could see her room and noted with relief that it appeared to be untouched, the Do Not Disturb sign still in place.

She still wanted to know why the hinges had been oiled.

Stepping out of the car, she followed slowly, her eyes scanning the area. While she'd noticed Brock doing the same thing, she couldn't help her own perusal.

It was kind of spooky the way she felt constantly

watched. Night was coming and she wondered what it might bring. Danger? A peaceful few hours of rest?

Or another threat telling her to leave town?

Brock opened his door and they stepped inside. He pulled his laptop from beneath the mattress and Gisella bit back a grin.

"What?" he asked when he looked up.

She motioned to the computer. "That's where I keep mine, too."

"And hang the Do Not Disturb sign on the door?"

"Absolutely."

"I don't need any sticky-fingered cleaning lady messing with anything. Although after what happened with your room, I'm tempted to keep it in the car with me." He powered it up.

She laughed. "After what happened to your car, that's the last place I'd keep it."

He shot her a mock frown. "Cute." Then he turned serious again. "This may take a few minutes. You're welcome to get that swim in if you want."

Longing hit her. The desire to slice through the water, feel it rushing over her, numbing her mind to everything except pushing her body to the limit… "Naw, I'm fine."

He raised a brow. "You're a pretty good actress. I almost believed that. As soon as I have the information, I'll bring it out to you. Now, go."

She shifted. "You're sure?"

"I'm sure. Just pay attention to your surroundings this time, huh?"

He didn't have to say it again. Fifteen minutes, twenty tops, was all she needed. A few laps and a quick change of clothes and she'd feel refreshed and ready to figure out where to go next with this case.

In record time, she'd changed into her swimsuit. Throwing her clothes over it, she grabbed her jacket and headed toward the covered pool area that was next to the office.

As she stepped into the enclosed area, she breathed in the familiar scent of chlorine, felt the humidity smack her in the face, and she smiled. The sound of the pump gurgled and Gisella felt herself relax.

A young woman with a toddler sat at one of the white plastic chairs. She'd pulled off the swimmies and now dried the little one's hair. They exchanged nods but Gisella breathed a happy sigh as the two left a few moments later.

She had the place to herself.

Entering the changing room, she left her clothes hanging on the pegs then reentered the pool area. Her blood hummed as she noted the depth of her end.

Eight feet.

Gisella dove in and felt the rush of water sluice over her. She surfaced and started swimming freestyle.

One lap.

Two.

Three.

She felt energized, the stresses of her work washing away as she stroked to the wall, flipped and pushed off to head back in the other direction.

How many laps did she have time for until Brock came looking for her?

She promised not to be long and she wouldn't. Just a few more.

She really needed to call her father. Let him vent for a while, rant about how she was sending her mother to an early grave and then she wouldn't have to worry about it for another week or two.

Not that she intentionally hurt her family. She would have thought her father, of all people, would have understood.

But he didn't. At least he said he didn't but sometimes, on the rare occasions that she made it home to visit, she thought she saw something in his eyes that showed he did.

And then the phone calls would come and she would tell herself she just imagined it.

Two more laps and she'd get out.

Maybe three.

She swam, feeling loose. Free.

And then the next time she surfaced…

…it was dark.

She gasped, bolted upright and realized she was in the deeper end of the pool.

Gisella froze in the water as best she could while still staying afloat. Her ears tuned in to the smallest sound. Her eyes swiveled, trying to pierce the darkness. Faint light filtered in through the tiny windows lining the top of the roof, but it wasn't enough to make out if someone was there, hiding in the shadows.

She hadn't heard anyone enter, but she'd been so focused on swimming…

A scrape.

Her heart thudded and she whirled toward the sound.

Nothing.

No. Wait. A shadow? Slight movement to her left?

Someone had turned the lights out and was now up to no good. Her head swiveled, her already pounding pulse picked up speed, now fueled by adrenaline.

Which way should she go?

The shallow end?

Stay in the deep?

She felt exposed. As though the person in the shadows could see her. But that was impossible. If she couldn't see him, he couldn't see her. Right?

Wrong. The faint lights under the water probably illuminated her form nicely for someone looking down into the water.

She paddled toward the end of the pool, placed her hands on the edge…

…and felt the cold snap of handcuffs encircle one wrist.

"Hey! Brock, if that's you trying to teach me another lesson, it's not funny."

She could see his legs now, grabbed on to one. He kicked out with the other and caught her in the shoulder. Gisella couldn't stop the pained yelp that escaped her and she let go. That wasn't Brock.

Something crashed into the water behind her and she felt herself being dragged beneath the surface. Pulling in one last minute breath, she fought against the force determined to land her on the bottom of the pool.

She went under.

Panic flooded through her as she realized the handcuff attached to her wrist was also connected to…what? Her trembling fingers fumbled to feel, eyes squinted trying to see in the dim underwater lights.

A chain.

She yanked.

But whatever weight was attached to the other end of the chain was too heavy.

Terror caused her heart to stutter and her lungs to strain.

Gisella dove after the weight that was now settled on the bottom.

She tugged.

It moved.

But not enough.

She couldn't lift it and she couldn't get out of the cuffs.

Lights prickled behind her eyes.

She had to breathe!

But if she did, she would drown.

If she didn't, she would pass out and drown anyway.

Brock! Where are you?

God, help me, please.

FIFTEEN

Brock glanced at his watch. Gisella had been gone a good ten minutes. She'd asked for fifteen. He'd give her a little more time then take the information down to her.

What little there was.

Chris Locke had come up clean.

Restless, he gave another glance at his watch and decided to go tell Gisella they needed to go another direction in the case. Right now, Jasper West seemed to be their best hope in finding who was the main boss with the Lions of Texas.

The thought didn't thrill him.

He grabbed his room key and headed out toward the pool. Opening the door, he paused as he glanced around, letting his eyes adjust to the sudden darkness.

Where were the lights?

Where was Gisella?

Foreboding chilled him.

"Gisella?" His voice echoed around him.

A door opened and a figure slipped out, shutting the door behind him.

Brock started to go after him then looked at the water, thought he saw…bubbles? A ripple? He couldn't tell.

Moving closer to get a better look, all senses on high alert, Brock made out a dark shape at the bottom of the pool.

And he knew.

Without thought, he kicked off his shoes, pulled off the heavy cable knit sweater that would drag him down and dove in.

Blinded by the darkness, he used his hands to feel for her. The tips of his fingers grazed hair. He snagged the strands, allowing them to guide him.

She whirled, fight and determination in her eyes. When she saw it was him, relief.

Then he saw her mouth open and she sucked in water. Thrashing, she fought whatever held her.

Oh, God, help. The prayer filtered through his mind even as he slid his hands under her arms to pull her up.

She didn't budge.

Her eyes bulged in fear and with the need to breathe.

She was getting ready to pass out and they both knew it. He could see it in her face. He didn't know how long she'd already been down there, but knew he only had a minute or two to get her up to air.

Sliding his hand down her arm, his fingers encountered the metal enclosed around her wrist.

His lungs sent out warning signals.

Brock's foot became entangled in something. Hard. Metal.

A chain?

He let go of Gisella and grasped it. His brain quickly calculated that it was about two feet long. How much time did he have? Not long. Her eyes closed and he knew if she hadn't passed out yet, she was close to it.

His fingertips scraped across something hard. Rough.

Concrete.

He pulled and it moved. Could he swim up with it?

God! I need some help! Please! Don't let her die.

Bunching his muscles, he grasped the block and pushed off the bottom of the pool. The block dragged him back. He needed another plan. Gisella stirred. Brock grabbed her wrist and pulled it close to get a look at what encircled it.

One ring on a handcuff.

Elated, he shoved his hand into his pocket and pulled out his key. Inserting it into the lock, he twisted it. The cuff fell off. Wrapping one arm at the base of her throat in a lifeguard hold, he shot for the surface.

Dots appeared before his eyes, and his lungs screamed for air. But he was almost there. Breaking through, he pulled in a much needed breath and swam for the shallow end, pulling Gisella behind him.

As soon as he could stand, he pulled her up. Placing her on the edge of the pool, he hoisted himself out and fitted his lips over hers. He blew and watched to see if her chest rose.

It did. *Come on, Gisella, breathe! God, I need Your help!*

He blew again, his fingers searching for a pulse.

It beat steady, so she didn't need chest compressions, just air.

Another breath and she wheezed a gasp. He turned her head and she spewed the water she'd swallowed and replaced it with life-giving oxygen.

"That's it. Breathe, darlin', breathe."

She coughed again. Spit some more.

He wiped her face with his hand and she blinked open her eyes. Dragged in another desperate gasp.

"Come on. We've got to get you to a hospital."

"No," she whispered. "I'm okay."

He snorted in disbelief. "Uh, I don't think so. You could have all sorts of complications."

Her head lolled to the side. He didn't care what she wanted. She was getting checked out by a doctor. In El Paso.

As soon as he retrieved the evidence. "I'll be right back."

Brock swam to the deep end, dived down and grasped the chain with the block attached. It was heavy. Letting go of the chain, he grasped the block and shoved off the bottom, working his way back toward Gisella. Mimicking an astronaut walking on the moon, he made his way toward the shallow end.

Heaving himself back out of the pool, he grabbed the large beach towel she'd thrown over the chair and draped it over her.

Gisella coughed again and this time it seemed to bring her back around. Sitting up, she pulled the edges of the towel together at her throat and sucked in another deep breath.

"I'm okay. You got here fast."

"I was restless and decided to come after you. Come on, we can be at the hospital in less than thirty minutes."

Tears leaked from her eyes and she shifted away from him. "Just give me a minute."

Reading her expression, he slid an arm around her. "Hey. Don't be embarrassed. That was a close one."

Leaning into him, she nodded against his shoulder and he felt his heart thump into overdrive.

Lifting her head, she met his gaze, searched his eyes and must have been okay with whatever she saw there. "Thanks," she whispered.

"You're welcome." He cleared his throat. "And hey, we're definitely even now."

Her lips curved into a reluctant smile. "I guess whoever did this is probably long gone by now."

"No doubt. I heard someone leave as I got here. He slipped out the side door. I started to go after him, but saw you." Brock found himself unable to tear his gaze away from this woman who was becoming more special to him with each passing moment.

His partner, Paul, flashed briefly through his mind. The man's grief, his inability to deal with his girlfriend's death all crashed into his consciousness.

Clearing his throat, he moved back slightly and Gisella furrowed her brow. "Well, I'm glad you saw me." She sighed. "Let me change and we'll go report this little incident to the office manager. See if there are any working cameras on this side of the building and if they picked up anything."

He nodded and helped her up. She gave another hacking cough and Brock frowned. "I really think you should at least get checked out."

She waved him off and entered the changing room.

Two minutes later, she was out, dressed in her

winter clothes. Brock had wrapped the concrete block in a towel, protecting it against his fingerprints. As soon as he got back to his car, he'd bag it properly.

He looked at his dripping outfit. "I'm going to get changed, too. Why don't you wait for me in your room? I'll knock when I'm ready." He gave another rueful look at his weapon. "And I have to dry and clean my gun again."

"Okay." She held up the wet bathing suit. "I need to hang this somewhere to dry anyway."

Together they headed toward the rooms.

Brock turned at the last minute to watch her disappear through the door.

His stomach churned at the thought of how close he'd come to losing her. So close it made him nauseated. Closing his eyes, he pulled in a long breath.

And made a vow.

No matter what it took, he'd make sure she stayed safe.

An uncomfortable feeling hit him as though someone taunted him saying, "Right. Just like Paul kept the woman he loved safe."

Shoving that aside, he decided to double up his guard and not let her out of his sight until this case was finished.

He also decided to keep that to himself as he felt quite sure Gisella wouldn't be on the same page with him in that book.

SIXTEEN

After calling Ben to let him know what had happened, Gisella gave another racking cough and bit her lip as she pondered their next move. Ben and Brock wanted her to go to the hospital. She wanted to wrap up this case.

Brock had cleaned his extra weapon and wanted to give the one that got dunked another good cleaning before carrying it again. He shrugged when Gisella expressed her concern. "After the deal with Lenny, I decided having a spare might not be a bad idea." He pulled up his pant leg and she spied the small weapon strapped to his ankle. "Fortunately, I didn't have it on me when we went swimming."

Gisella watched him lower his pant leg back over the weapon and decided he was right. The way things were going in this town, that might actually be an excellent idea.

She rubbed a hand down her face. "Let's take a look at the camera focused on the pool. I noticed it the night someone blew up your car."

"Okay, sounds good as long as you're sure you feel all right."

She didn't bother to reassure him again. Instead, she made her way to the office. Brock's steps echoed behind her.

Entering the office, she noticed the clerk, Steve, behind the desk wiping down the computer. She asked, "Do you have some ibuprofen? I've got a headache and I'm out."

Steve stopped his cleaning and opened the cabinet behind him. It creaked upon opening and he frowned. After handing her the small packet with two pills and a bottle of water from the small refrigerator to the left, he reached under the desk and pulled out a bottle of WD-40. Spraying the hinges, he tested the door until it stopped its annoying squeak.

Gisella opened the packet and popped the two pills, swigged them down with the water and froze.

"Did you oil the hinges in my room?"

Steve stilled, his jaw went tight. "Yeah. Your door was squeaking."

"How would you know that?" she asked softly.

"The maid told me."

Gisella set her water on the counter. She wanted her hands free. Brock stilled, watching her. She didn't have time to fill him in on what she was thinking. If she did, she'd lose her opportunity with the man.

"I'm sorry, Steve, but the maid couldn't have told you about the door because I put the Do Not Disturb sign on it. She hasn't been in the room."

The man's eyes flicked from her to the exit door. Gisella's gut tightened. The only reason he'd do that was because he felt the need to run.

"Steve," Brock said, "is there something you need to tell us?"

Steve gave a nervous laugh. "I don't know what you're talking about. Why are you making such a big deal out of me oiling your hinges? That's my job, you know? To take care of this place."

"And you do a great job. But I still want to know about the hinges in my room."

"Look, I just remembered that the last customer who stayed in your room complained about the door. I didn't want it bothering you so I oiled them. Simple as that." His hand slapped the counter.

Gisella studied him. "You've just told me two different stories. And I don't believe either one."

Steve glared and crossed his arms across his chest. That was fine with her. As long as she could see them, he wasn't reaching for a weapon.

She looked him in the eye. A muscle jumped in his cheek and she followed her gut feeling. "I think you let Jasper West in my room to leave that message on my shower curtain. And when you heard the squeaky door, you decided to come back and oil it."

"What?" he exploded. His eyes hardened and his

hands once again slapped the counter only to curl into fists. "Why would you accuse me of something like that?" He lifted one fist and shook it in her direction. "Because I have prison tats?"

"No," Gisella stated calmly, "because it makes sense. You have something bordering an obsessive compulsive disorder when it comes to cleaning, don't you?"

Surprise flickered and he didn't deny it. Then he shrugged. "So what? I was on the cleaning crew at the prison. It helped pass the time."

"Those hinges would have driven you nuts from the time you heard them to the time you got there to oil them. If the last person in that room complained about the noise, you would have oiled the hinges immediately. I don't think you even knew about them—until you heard them when you let Jasper in."

Fury built in the man's eyes and Gisella knew she'd scored a bull's-eye with her deduction. Brock shifted away from her, moving to the left of the counter. "Why don't you come out from behind there, sir, and let's sit over here and talk?"

Steve moved as though to comply—until his right hand dropped out of sight. Brock had his weapon in his hand only a fraction of a second before Gisella had hers.

"Don't do it," Brock ordered. "Take your hand off the weapon."

Gisella noticed him watching the clerk using the

mirror behind him. Steve froze and Gisella scrambled over the counter. She grabbed his arms and pulled them behind his back to cuff him. Breathing hard with the surge of adrenaline, she started coughing.

And coughing.

Brock simply covered the man until she recovered. Steve turned his head and smirked. "What's the matter? Can't breathe underwater?"

Brock's indrawn breath sounded harsh to her ringing ears. "Ignore him, Brock," she gasped. "At least that answers one question."

"Now for the second," Brock growled. "Was it you who let Jasper into Gisella's room?"

"I want a lawyer."

They called the sheriff and after expressing his disgust at the trouble they seemed to find, they spent the next two hours dealing with Steve's surly attitude and his lawyer, the same one who'd represented Jasper West.

Surprisingly enough, Steve seemed to be more concerned about getting someone to cover the desk at the hotel than about the fact that he was being arrested for helping Jasper leave his threatening message, and for the attempted murder of a Texas Ranger.

Gisella and Brock sat in an office at the police station filling out paperwork on the events of the night.

"I wonder if he's also responsible for blowing up my car?" Brock muttered.

"Probably. I have a feeling those cameras that he claimed were broken, aren't." She typed the last sentence and pressed print. "But the crime scene unit from El Paso is at the hotel now. Hopefully, with a little pressure from Ben, they'll make this case a priority and get everything processed as fast as possible." The concrete block complete with handcuffs and chain had been bagged and given to the crime scene unit upon arrival. The sheriff had come to pick up Steve, taken their report—and no doubt grumbled all the way back to his office. Once the proper authorities had arrived, Gisella and Brock made their way to the sheriff's office to finish paperwork and question Steve. "I'm done, how about you?"

"Almost."

"Honestly, you'd think one of them would offer up a full confession for a lighter sentence or some kind of deal with the District Attorney," she muttered. "But nothing. They're both closed up tighter than a clam. It makes me wonder."

"I know. They're either deathly afraid of whoever they're protecting or…"

"They expect that person to get them off with only a slap on the wrist."

She sighed and coughed, her lungs burning. But there was one more thing she wanted to do before calling it a night. "I want to drive out to the border station and check out the crossing." She glanced at him. "I mean, we know the drugs aren't coming over right in front of the Border Patrol's eyes, but maybe by seeing the area, we can kind of get a feel for it."

"For possible entry points?"

She nodded. "We're sure not getting anywhere talking to people around here. The sheriff, with some help from the state police, is taking care of Ina's murder. The crime scene unit has the hotel. Steve and Jasper aren't talking. However, the sheriff said they found one interesting thing in Steve's possession.

"What's that?"

"A key to a rental cabin on the lake here in Boot Hill. Had the tag on the ring and everything. Very easy to track down."

"What would he need a rental cabin on the lake for? Does he live there?"

"No. That's the strange thing. He lives behind the hotel."

Brock shook his head. "Weird."

"Definitely." She rubbed the back of her neck.

"What?"

"While we're waiting on Jasper or Steve to decide to talk, why don't we visit the border crossing?"

Brock frowned at her. "I think you should probably rest. You almost drowned."

She frowned right back at him. "I'm fine." She

was tired and wanted nothing more than to crawl in bed and sleep for a few hours but the image of her dead fellow Ranger and friend, Captain Pike, kept her going.

"Something's bothering me," she murmured.

"What's that?"

"How did Steve know I would go swimming at that particular time? It was a total impulse swim."

Brock nodded, not surprised at her question. She narrowed her eyes. "You've already thought about that, huh?"

"Yeah."

"And your conclusion?"

"He was watching us. 24/7. Those little security monitors behind the desk probably made his job pretty easy."

Gisella blew out a breath and muttered, "Thanks for the confirmation."

"You've been thinking the same?"

"Of course. And I don't think he's the only one. I think whoever doesn't want us here has paid eyes all over this town." She paused then shook her head. "But it doesn't matter. We're here to do a job and watched or not, we're going to do it."

A slow smile spread across his face. "I like the way you think."

Gisella stifled the urge to giggle. Instead, she scoffed, "Since when?" He shot her a mock-wounded look. She ignored it. "Seriously, all kidding aside, I just want to ride out to the border and look around. It's not far, just a couple of miles."

Still looking like he didn't approve, he nodded. "I know where it is. I've been out that way a few times."

"Great. Let's go."

He blew out an aggravated sigh. "Fine, but if I think you're suffering any side effects, we're coming back."

She rolled her eyes and waved him to the vehicle. She'd just keep quiet about the fact that fatigue pulled at her with an insistent tug. She also keep to herself the fact that her chest hurt from coughing.

But she was breathing fine. She could make it to the border for a look around.

Brock rubbed his chin and frowned as he drove. "I was thinking that it's possible Steve had something else in mind with that block of cement and handcuffs and just lucked out at seeing you walk to the pool."

"What do you mean?"

"I agree someone is watching the hotel. It might have even been Steve. Could be just a kid being paid to watch our comings and goings who reports in every once in a while. However, there's a lake on the edge of town. Steve had a key to a cabin on the lake. I'm guessing whoever rigged that block of cement had something else in mind."

"Like sending one of us to the bottom of the lake?"

"Maybe. I mean, he couldn't count on the fact that you would go swimming or that you would be alone when you went. I think this was a crime of opportunity. He could see on the monitor that the pool was empty. He could also see you were alone when you entered the building. He grabbed his stuff and took advantage of the moment. He probably thought, why not use the pool instead of the lake?"

Gisella pondered his reasoning and couldn't find fault with it. Until Steve decided to talk, it sounded like a plausible explanation.

Gisella's phone rang. "Hello, Ben."

"How are you feeling?"

"I'm all right. Tired, but glad to be alive."

"The crime scene team found something interesting in all of the clerk's cleaning supplies."

"What'd they find?"

"Chloroform."

She frowned. "Chloroform? Okay. What else?"

"They've bagged the weapon he had behind the counter and they found a stash of cash in the safe. State police are questioning the rest of the hotel guests, but my bet is the cash was payment for getting rid of you."

Gisella blew out a breath. "All right."

"And then there was the email."

"That said?"

"How Steve was to sneak into your room at night, use the chloroform and dump you in the lake hand-cuffed to the concrete block."

Her stomach hurt. But for the grace of God and her putting it all together with the hinges… She shuddered. "Did you find who sent the email?"

"It came from one of the library computers. The account was bogus, listed to a John Doe."

She grimaced. "Okay, thanks for the update, Ben."

"Take care. And watch your back. Just because this particular guy is taken care of, doesn't mean someone else isn't ready to take his place."

"Yeah." She hung up and filled Brock in.

Brock's jaw formed into a block of concrete. "So those oiled hinges were to serve another purpose."

"Looks like it. Without them squeaking, depend-ing on how soundly I was sleeping, I would have been a pretty easy target." She pictured it in her mind and gave another shiver.

"How did you put it all together? What made you pick up on the OCD stuff?"

For a minute she didn't answer then she blew out a sigh and said, "My brother had OCD. I think that's why he turned to drugs. To help him deal with the stress of it all. My parents wouldn't admit that he had a problem so there was no getting him the kind of help he needed."

Brock's warm hand reached out and covered hers. "I'm sorry."

She squeezed his fingers, grateful for his presence, thankful that he'd found her in time. "Thank you."

Arriving to the border crossing, still sitting in the car, Gisella looked at the fence. Part of a two-thousand-mile border fence erected a few years ago, it was an effort by Homeland Security to halt illegal alien entry into the United States—or at least cut down on the numbers.

But it didn't stop all of the drug runners, illegal aliens and possible terrorists. The cameras and alarms weren't infallible and people still managed to get over the fence. Her question was: How were they consistently getting the drugs across the border and into Boot Hill—and beyond—without being caught?

This was what she'd been assigned to figure out. This was the job she loved, her calling in life. And she was just now getting around to really doing what needed to be done. Why? Because she'd been occupied with one incident after another. From Brock's car exploding to Ina's murder to her near drowning.

And she realized something.

"It's all been a distraction," she whispered.

Brock looked at her. "What do you mean?"

The more she thought about it, the more it made sense. "Everything that's happened has been to keep us from coming here—and my guess is, if one or both of us ended up dead, so much the better."

His right brow lifted as though she spoke a language he didn't understand. "Seriously, think about it." Earnestly, she held out a hand as though to compel him. "We never made any secret about why we were here."

He cocked his head and looked at her. "True."

"So if the drugs are coming over the border—and we know they are, even if we can't prove it, yet— then all the smugglers had to do was keep us from coming here and snooping around."

Brock rubbed his chin. "Well, when you put it like that…"

"Exactly." She pulled on her gloves and got out of the car, still processing everything. "Let's walk the fence, okay?"

He climbed out after her. "Sure."

"Hey, Ranger, what are you two doing here?"

Niles Vernon.

Gisella turned to see the man bundled up in a heavy Border Patrol jacket, warm hat and gloves. She flashed him a smile. "Just thought I'd see what the border crossing was like down here." She could see her breath hover in the air when she talked.

It was cold today. In Boot Hill, the average low temperature in January hovered around freezing. Her lungs still felt tortured and she coughed in an effort to clear them. It helped. Some.

Niles shrugged. "Like any other border crossing, I reckon. When you've seen one, you've seen them all."

Brock and Niles shook hands. Gisella started walking, her eyes probing for holes in the fence, a break in it. Anything that would explain how—and where—the drugs were coming in.

Brock came up behind her. "See anything?"

"Nothing."

"What exactly are you looking for?" Niles questioned.

Gisella sighed and gave another cough. "I'm not sure. I guess I thought I'd just come down here and..." She waved a hand in dismissal.

"Hey," Brock interrupted, "is that part the graveyard where we found Ina?"

Niles shoved his gloved hands into his coat pockets. "Yeah. It's the only graveyard in Boot Hill and it backs up to the fence." Gisella stepped forward to get a better look. Large bushes lined the chain-link fence and she realized that the night Ina had been killed, she'd been so focused on the area surrounding the murder, she'd not paid attention to how close they'd been to the border.

Niles blew out a sigh. "Well, you showed up at the right time. Come on this way and I'll show you where I think some people have been sneaking across."

Gisella pulled her attention away from the graveyard and followed Niles. Brock brought up the rear once again. He'd been awfully quiet. She looked back at him. "Are you all right?"

"Yes, I'm fine. Just processing everything. How about you?"

Instead of giving him a pat answer, she said honestly, "I'm tired."

He placed an arm around her shoulders. "As soon as we're done here, let's head back to the hotel and you can crash. I'll stay on duty tonight."

"On duty?"

Brock shook his head and gave a forlorn sigh. "Something's bound to happen. Might as well be expecting it."

She gave him a light punch to his ribs and he smiled, catching her gaze and holding it. "You're…"

"You guys coming?" Niles interrupted.

Brock gave a grimace and Gisella's heart beat faster at the thought of what he might have been getting ready to say.

Placing a hand at her back, Brock guided her toward Niles. Gisella watched the man disappear around the side of a small building.

As she rounded it, she found him down on one knee pointing at the fence. "Found this just a little while ago." Gisella cocked her head wondering what he was talking about. She didn't see anything unusual.

Reaching out, he snagged part of the fence and pulled. A section came off in his hand and he held it up, leaving a gaping hole, big enough for a large man to crawl through.

Brock let out a low whistle. "Clever."

"Yep. And there's no camera on that side of the building that hits this corner. They found themselves a sweet spot and went at it. Any further away, and the cameras would have caught it. Right under our noses, and we can't see a thing."

"But how did you not see someone approaching with the tools to do this kind of thing?" Gisella asked.

His jaw tightened. "Good question." His gaze flicked toward the other building. The one where other agents worked and pedestrians could cross through the opening after providing the appropriate credentials. "A camera's being installed tomorrow to take care of this little problem. My guess is before using this for the first time, someone camped out on the inside and learned the routine of the station. Took notes, etc. Then all he had to do was figure out the times that would work best to sneak out. Times such as shift changes, meetings when there are fewer agents on duty." He shrugged. "Pretty easy doings, if you ask me."

"All right," she said. "Let's get this hole plugged." She felt her energy drain to near-sub-zero levels and looked at Brock. "It's getting late. Why don't we head back into town and grab a bite to eat?"

His sharp gaze showed concern. She hadn't fooled him with her casual suggestion. "Sure. Let's do that." He turned to Niles and shook the man's hand. "We'll catch you later."

Gisella climbed into the car and wilted.

Brock leaned over and brushed a wisp of hair from her face, leaving a tingling sensation where he touched. "You're pushing yourself too hard."

"I have to," she whispered. Her phone rang. She looked at the ID and sighed. Her dad. Maybe she should answer it.

The sun had disappeared five minutes ago. Brock cranked the car and turned on the headlights.

She clicked to answer the phone. "Hi, Dad."

"Gisella, finally. You haven't learned how to dial a number yet?"

"Ha ha, Dad. And I did call and leave you a message."

He grunted. "When you knew we'd be out of the house and eating dinner with friends."

Gisella had no argument for that. He was right. "I'm on a case so I've been a little busy."

"Tell me about the case." She heard the eager

anticipation in his voice and knew being a Ranger would be in his blood until he died.

"I can't right now. Maybe in a few weeks, okay?"

"Sure." Disappointment rang. Then he changed the subject. "Your mother wants to know…"

"When I'm going to quit my dangerous job, come home and let her teach me how to cook, right?" She was so tired of this. Gisella flicked a glance at Brock. He didn't even try to hide his curiosity as he listened with rapt attention. She resisted sticking her tongue out at him. She'd chosen to answer the call in his presence.

"Yes, yes, of course," her father was saying. "Gisella." He lowered his voice. "Your mother needs you here."

Alarm shot through her. "Is she sick?" He hesitated and she firmed her jaw. "Dad, shoot straight with me. Is she sick or is it another one of her ploys to get me to come home?"

A sigh filtered through the line. "A ploy. I think."

Gisella closed her eyes. At least he wouldn't lie to her. "All right. Tell her as soon as I finish this case, I'll come see her. And stay a while. Deal?"

"I'll tell her."

They hung up and Gisella groaned.

"So, your parents aren't supportive of your career, huh?"

She didn't bother opening her eyes. "Like I said

before, they've lost one child; they're not real keen on losing another."

Like to drowning. She shuddered.

"Are they hounding you about grandchildren yet?"

She laughed. "Of course. My mother mostly. When she gets the chance." Her smile faded. "I try not to give her the chance very often."

A hand rested on her left shoulder, another cupped her jaw. Her eyes popped open and she looked at him, light from the moon illuminating his intent. She had no chance to react before he leaned over and captured her lips with his. Gisella froze in shock for a brief moment, then let herself adjust to the moment. Her stomach did that weird swooping thing and her heart stuttered in her chest. His left thumb caressed her jaw—and she slammed back to earth with a thud.

Pulling back, she covered her lips with a hand. "Brock, we can't..." she whispered.

He held up a hand to stop her words. "I know. That might not have been the smartest move I've ever made, but I..." He stopped.

"You what?"

"You fascinate me. You have from the moment you saved my life." He swallowed hard. "What is it about you that I'm so drawn to?"

Shock made her catch her breath. She'd never had

a man express himself so openly with her. Then pain clouded his eyes and he looked away.

"Hey." She grabbed his hand. "Look at me."

At first he didn't respond and she wondered if he would. Then slowly his head turned and his eyes made contact.

She said, "What was that I just saw in your eyes? What are you thinking?"

Those sky-blue eyes clouded over. "It doesn't matter. Nothing."

"Don't lie to me," she said. Although her tone was mild, her rebuke rang loud and clear.

A sigh slipped from him. "I…had a partner once, a very short-lived pairing."

"Did he get killed?" Her heart clenched at the thought.

But he shook his head. "No. Before we were partners, Paul was paired up with a female agent."

Gisella studied him. This was really hard for him to tell her. She decided to wait him out, see if he would finish the story.

He swallowed hard. "Paul fell in love with her and she was the one killed."

"Oh, Brock, I'm so sorry."

"He lasted three more months on the job after that and quit."

Looking away, he rubbed his eyes then caught her gaze again. The moon seemed to sharpen the angles on his face, cause his eyes to glow. But it was his words that she was most interested in. "Why are you telling me this?"

"Because I'm falling for you and I swore I'd never get involved with someone I worked with."

Gisella felt a pang of joy followed swiftly by sorrow. "I see."

So, why had he just kissed her?

Brock slapped the wheel and she jumped. He clenched his fist. "I'm sorry, Gisella, I don't go around just kissing women—not even when I'm attracted to them. I'm not like that. With you, though," his voice lowered, "there's something different about you. Special."

What did she say to that? One minute she wanted to punch him, the next she wished he'd lean over and kiss her again.

"Brock…"

"No, let me finish."

Gisella bit her lip.

Sucking in a deep breath, as though gathering his courage, he finally looked at her again. Really studied her. "I'm going to sound like a real wimp telling you this, but…you scare me. And—" another deep breath "—I'm not sure what to do about that."

She swallowed hard then narrowed her eyes at him. He wasn't the only one scared of the feelings running between them. "I understand what you're saying, Brock. I really do. However, until you figure out which way you're going to go with your feelings, then no more flirting, no more kisses. Just business, okay? I don't need you messing with my head—or my heart."

His confession stunned her. And reinforced what she'd figured all along.

He wasn't someone she was interested in falling for. She didn't need someone who didn't know what he wanted. Or one who was too wrapped up in being afraid to love. From now on, she'd be professional, kind—but distant.

She didn't like the fact that the thought caused her heart to ache—and a little voice to say it was too late.

He flinched. "Gisella, that's not what I meant..."

"I'm exhausted. Just drive, Brock, okay?"

Leaning her head back against the seat rest, she shut her eyes, closing out the world around her—and the man next to her.

SEVENTEEN

Seven hours later, after skipping supper and sleeping pretty well considering she woke coughing every so often, Gisella blinked as the sun peeked around the edges of her curtains and the beat of helicopter blades came from overhead. Taking a deep breath, she waited for a coughing spasm to hit her and felt relief when it didn't.

She used her palms to scrub away the last dregs of sleep and realized she'd fallen asleep over the little black book with all the numbers and letters she was still trying to decode.

Setting it on the end table, she took a deep breath. No lingering effects from her attempted murder yesterday.

What still bothered her was the conversation she'd had with Brock in the car.

And the kiss.

She could definitely fall in love with a man like that, her heart insisted. Her mind shouted warnings loud and clear. He had his own issues about her and her job. She certainly didn't need to add that stress to her life.

But she found herself thinking about the idea of what it would be like to have him in her life on a permanent basis.

It would be crazy. They'd probably argue about everything. But their minds worked amazingly alike, too.

Definitely crazy.

She gave a wry smile. And to think she hadn't liked him just a few days ago. It was incredible how first impressions could be so wrong, snap judgments so unreliable.

I'm sorry, Lord, for judging him before getting to know him. Brock's a good guy. Just help me guard my heart, please?

Swinging her legs over the side of the bed, she rose and headed for the shower. No doubt Brock would soon be knocking on her door, ready for breakfast and for questioning Boot Hill residents.

Determination sat heavy on her. She was going to find how those drugs were coming in—one way or another.

As she pulled her hair up into a no-nonsense bun, her phone rang. Exiting the bathroom, she snatched it from the nightstand and glanced at the caller ID.

"Hi, Ben."

"Just got your message. Are you all right?" he barked.

"I'm fine. No lasting effects, I don't think."

"Do I need to send help? Levi and Evan can be there within a few hours. Even faster than that by helicopter."

"No. Don't pull them from what they're working on. Brock and I've got it covered. We're just having to be a little more vigilant than we planned." An understatement, but she knew Levi and Evan were working hard to uncover who had sent threatening letters targeting the Alamo anniversary celebration, and making sure security was as tight as it could be.

"Don't end up dead on me, Gisella."

"No, sir, that's not in my plans. And hopefully not God's, either." She changed the subject. "Have you gotten anything out of Jorge Cantana?" Dr. Cantana had been arrested after trying to kill Quin Morton, the man still hospitalized in San Antonio.

"No, nothing. He's got two small daughters that he's trying to protect with his silence. He knows if he talks, the Lions will kill them. As a result, he refuses to talk other than to say he *can't* talk. But he's one of the upper echelon of the Lions. We're making progress, Gisella. We just need to know where the drugs are coming from."

"I know, Ben. The two guys we arrested, Jasper and Steve, still aren't talking, but we're working on it."

"I know you are. All right. Keep me in the loop." He paused. "Corinna says hello."

She smiled. Ben's fiancée had been Gisella's roommate for a short time. "Give her my love."

"Always. Take care and let me know if you need anything. I'm going to put pressure on the lab to get that cement block and handcuffs processed ASAP."

"Thanks, Ben."

They hung up and Gisella rubbed at the headache that had just made itself known over her right eye. She wasn't holding her breath on the lab finding anything. In the desperate struggle to escape the cuffs, she and Brock had both had their fingerprints all over the items and had probably smudged or covered up anything there.

But Ben would try anyway.

A knock sounded at her door and she pocketed her cell phone, hid her laptop and grabbed her gun.

Instead of using the peephole provided, she pushed a small amount of curtain aside and looked out.

Brock.

Opening the door, she shoved her weapon into the holster on her hip. "Good morning."

He smiled, crinkling the corners of his eyes. Her heart thumped and she nearly groaned out loud. Her response to this man made her "just business between us" statement from the night before a mockery.

Telling herself to put a lid on her emotions, she smiled back, hoping it was cooler than the heat she felt in her cheeks. "Good morning."

His smile slipped a fraction. "Are you ready to see if Mr. West or Mr. Billings has anything to say this morning?"

"Absolutely. I hope a night in jail made one of them decide to cooperate."

"Let's find out."

Five minutes later, they walked into the jail.

Gisella immediately knew something was wrong. From the tense set to one deputy's shoulders to the grim look on the receptionist's face, they all advertised trouble. Grabbing the nearest person by the arm, she asked, "What happened?"

"Jasper West escaped and the sheriff's having a fit."

Gisella's gaze shot to Brock's and frustration curled through her. Every time she thought they were about to take one step forward, they were pushed two steps back.

"When? How?"

The tall worker nodded. "Here comes the sheriff. I'll let you talk to him." And then he was gone, no doubt anxious to escape the impending storm.

"Sheriff, what happened? Where's Jasper West?" Brock demanded.

Sheriff Johnston's tight lips drew tighter. "He's gone and I've got a deputy near death. He's been airlifted to the hospital in El Paso. His gun was stolen so West is armed."

The helicopter she'd heard this morning.

Gisella's stomach twisted again and her fingers curled into a fist by her side. Brock caught her eye and shook his head in disgust. "What about Steve Billings?"

Sheriff Johnston said, "He and West got into a fight. West managed to knock him out cold by the time my deputy arrived. Jasper jumped the deputy, grabbed his gun and lit out."

"This means Jasper was probably going to talk and Billings didn't like it," Brock growled.

"So Billings was going to beat him to a pulp but Jasper did a good job of defending himself."

"And when my deputy arrived, West acted like he was hurt. When my deputy checked on him, he got his head slammed against the floor. Locke found the two of them, the deputy and Billings, out cold on the floor." His lips twisted in disgust. "Locke!"

Chris looked up from the woman he was talking to. "Yes, sir?"

"You finish questioning the staff?"

"Almost."

"Anything we can do, Sheriff?" Brock asked.

"Stay out of my way." He glowered. "Ever since you two showed up, things have gone from bad to worse in this town."

With those words, he turned on his heel and headed for his office.

Gisella blew out a sigh. "Hmm. That went well."

"Yep."

She looked at him. "Something major is going on. I can feel it."

"Does this have anything to do with what you meant last night when you said everything that happened was meant to be a diversion?"

"Yes. Like I've said before, I just have this feeling that we're either supposed to be dead—which would be the preferable option for whoever has tried to kill me—or have our attention on something else."

"Something other than..."

"...the border," they said together.

He rubbed his chin in that endearingly masculine way he had. "I feel like a stakeout. How about you?"

"Hate 'em. But agree they're a necessary evil."

"Tonight?" he asked with a raised brow.

"Tonight."

Darkness fell swiftly, swallowing the remaining daylight with one big gulp. Once again, Brock found himself in close quarters with Gisella.

And not minding it one bit.

Unfortunately, he had a feeling he might have ruined any chance at a relationship with her because he'd let his fear rear its ugly head.

And yet he didn't want to be dishonest and lead her on, either.

His mind swirled. His heart thudded. He didn't want to admit it, but he knew out of all the women he'd dated and flirted with, Gisella was the one that he could easily lose his heart to.

And unless he got it together and got over the memory of Paul's experience, Brock knew he'd lose Gisella. For good.

The thought shot terror through him.

Could he let her go? He knew with certainty he didn't want to. But…

Could he get past his partner's bad experience and move on with someone who might get killed because she placed herself in dangerous situations every day?

He squirmed. He did the same with his job. Did he have a right to wish she would get a safe job while he continued doing what he loved?

Of course not.

So. Where did that leave him?

Swallowing hard, he came to a painful realization.

He couldn't keep her safe no matter how vehemently he vowed to do so.

Only God had that power. Humbled, he felt his throat swell with emotion. *I'm sorry I was arrogant enough to think that I could protect her on my own. I definitely need Your help, Lord.*

"What are you thinking?" Her quiet question from behind the binoculars she had glued to her eyes slammed into him.

"That I don't trust God nearly as much as I should." Where had that come from?

She startled in the dark and lowered the binoculars, her eyes wide. There was just enough light that he could make out her expression. Then she gave a small laugh. "Well, you're not the only one with that problem."

"What do you not trust Him with?" He was curious. Not once had she expressed doubt about the God he knew she loved.

Gisella grimaced. "Oh, I trust Him with it. You know, give my problems to Him. I just don't leave them with Him. I tend to take them back like I don't think He can handle them."

"Then give it back when it becomes too big for you again?"

She gave a short laugh. "Yes. Unfortunately. I know better. God can handle it. But I just sometimes…" She trailed off and lifted the binoculars again.

"What particular situation are you thinking of?"

"My family," she muttered.

"Ah."

"Yep."

"My parents are still together and I want to have a marriage like theirs one day." He needed a zipper on his mouth.

Once again he'd managed to shock her. Her eyes

flew wide and she gaped. Her expression put him on the defensive. "What?"

She shrugged. "I just didn't picture you as the marrying kind."

He frowned at her. "I'm not a playboy, Gisella."

This time she flushed. "I didn't say you were, I just…"

"Well, now you know. I want marriage and a family. One day."

"Soon?"

"Whenever it's supposed to happen, I suppose."

"Trusting God on that?"

He smiled, appreciating her humor. "Working on it." A pause. "More so now since the night you saved my hide from Lenny and his itchy trigger finger."

"Staring death in the face does cause one to put things in perspective."

Brock couldn't read her face now. "What have you put in perspective since your near drowning?"

Her brows rose in appreciation of his insight. "My relationship with my parents."

His cell phone rang and he grabbed it.

"Hello? Martin here."

"This is Sheriff Johnston. Where are you two?"

"Excuse me?"

"Niles and two other Border Patrol agents just brought in about ten illegals trying to cross the border and I thought I'd see if you two felt up to helping us process them. I'm short about three deputies tonight and one of the Border Patrol agents needs medical attention and is leaving."

"Well, sir, right now, Gisella and I are…" A loud crash sounded through the phone and Brock jerked it from his ear. The sheriff cursed then said, "One of the prisoners kicked a trash can across the room. If you can spare a couple of hours, I would appreciate it."

Brock hung up and relayed the message to Gisella.

A thoughtful look crossed her face. "We could, but my first priority is this case. Let's give it a while longer and see what turns up."

"Works for me." He held his hand out for the binoculars. "Want me to take a look?"

"Sure." She handed them over. As he took them, his palm grazed her fingers, sending goose bumps over his flesh. With a jolt, he realized that while he was physically attracted to this woman, the pull she had over him was more than that.

He admired her. Her softness laced with steel. Her determination to do her job. Her loyalty to her dead boss and fellow Rangers. Her willingness to admit that while she loved the Lord, she was human and could be besieged with doubts just like the next person.

Just like him.

He blinked and his phone rang again. His lips curved at the number. "Yes, Sheriff."

"Sorry I had to hang up there. So, you think you can give me a hand?"

He looked at Gisella. "The sheriff again."

She gave a disgusted look out the window. "Sure. There's nothing happening here anyway. Maybe my hunch was all wrong." She snapped her seat belt into place. "Tell him we're on our way."

Brock did and then pulled his laptop out to log in to the site that would allow him to input his information about the stakeout.

Gisella watched Brock enter his username then turned her head so he wouldn't think she was being nosey, trying to get his password or something.

BCM had been the first three letters he'd entered. "What's your middle name?" she asked.

He typed a few more letters then shut the computer off. He looked at her and grinned. "Cameron. Brock Cameron Martin, my lady. What's yours?"

Gisella grimaced. "Not telling."

He laughed. "Oh, come on, you can't say that and then expect me not to hound you about it."

She sighed and rolled her eyes. "Eldora."

One brow rose indicating his surprise. "Your parents did that to you on purpose?"

She choked a surprised laugh, then giggled and whacked him lightly on his arm. "Thanks a lot."

A sheepish grin covered his face. "Sorry."

Her heart flipped and she realized she was in deep despite his feelings about her dangerous job.

Immediately she berated herself. No more flirting, remember? Keep it cool and distant.

But she couldn't seem to help it. She liked him. Maybe even loved him. The thought of being without him in her life made her heart ache like someone was trying to remove it without anesthesia. Oh, boy. She took a deep breath. "Ready to go?"

"Yep."

Brock Cameron Martin.

BCM.

Initials.

Something niggled at the back of her mind, irritating her like a pebble in her shoe. What was it? What...

The initials in the little black book flashed at her. The initials on the grave plots on the map on the wall popped to mind. Excitement stirred. "Wait a minute."

"What?" He pulled out of the parking lot.

"That's it," she breathed. "I think I know where we need to go next."

"Where?"

"The morgue."

"Why?"

"Because sometimes dead people do tell tales."

EIGHTEEN

Brock just shot her a look and she realized he was waiting not so patiently for her to tell him what she was talking about. "Your initials sparked an idea. I'm going to call the sheriff back and tell him we have a little errand to run first."

"He's not going to be happy."

"He hasn't been happy since we showed up. Why change the status quo? But if I'm right about this, it'll make up for all the grief we've caused him."

After promising to be there as soon as possible, but not explaining what errand they had to do, she hung up and told Brock, "Go to the morgue, will you? I want to look at that map on the wall one more time."

"It's probably locked up." But he headed in that direction.

She frowned. "You're right. Let's stop by the diner and see if Pop is there. Maybe he can open it up for us."

Brock drove to the diner and Gisella hopped out of the car. "I'll be right back if you want to wait."

"Sure."

Entering the diner, she looked around and spotted Krista. Approaching her, Gisella asked, "Is Pop here?"

"In the back. You want me to get him?"

"Please."

Krista whirled to head toward Gisella who tapped her foot impatiently, her adrenaline surging at the thought of what this night might bring if her hunch was right.

Pop came out of the kitchen wiping his hands on his stained apron. Krista followed and began waiting tables again.

Gisella greeted him and made her request. "I just need to look at the map on the wall. Can you let me in for five minutes? Maybe not even that long."

The man eyed her for a brief moment then nodded. "Krista—" he waved the girl over once again "—get my keys and let these two in the morgue, will you? Make sure you lock up tight when you're done."

The girl's eyes went wide, but she didn't argue or ask questions. Her hostility seemed to have lessened since the last time she saw them. "Sure, Pop." Once again she disappeared into the back. Pop nodded as though to reassure himself he was doing the right thing.

"Thank you so much," Gisella said.

Krista returned within seconds, keys in her left hand.

They all climbed in the car and Brock drove them

the few blocks to the morgue. A single bulb glowed over the small porch that led up to the building.

Krista climbed out of the car. Her eyes glowing with excitement and curiosity, she took the lead and opened the door for them. Brock looked at Gisella. "After you."

Gisella stepped inside and made her way down the hallway to the small, but well-equipped area that served as the morgue and autopsy room.

Flipping on the light, she moved across the floor, her eyes landing on the wall-size map of the cemetery. Energy flowed through her, and her stomach dipped and rolled with adrenaline. Opening the book, she turned to the weird symbol on the last page and breathed, "It's a match."

Brock studied it over her shoulder. "Way to go, Gisella. Nice catch."

She looked at the map with the small boxes and their corresponding letters nestled inside them. "I'm most interested in the ones near the fence closest to the border," she muttered, then realized Krista stood watching them, taking in everything they were talking about.

Not wanting to discuss the case—and possibly sensitive information—in front of the girl, Gisella asked her to wait in the reception room.

Krista pouted a minute, then shrugged and did as asked.

After Krista disappeared down the hall, Gisella

pulled her phone out and snapped a picture of the map on the wall. Looking at Brock, she shrugged. "You never know. Might come in handy in the graveyard."

"Definitely."

In the little book, Gisella flipped back to the beginning and found the list of numbers and letters she and Brock had focused on initially.

"JZ, RP, QV. And the mixture of numbers and letters: 3149NJZ10724WRPQV. JZ, RP and QV all appear in that sequence, right?" Excitement hurried her words.

"Yep."

"What if the numbers are longitude and latitude and the N is north?"

"And the W is west?"

"Coordinates," she breathed. "But for what?"

Slowly, he nodded. "I think you're right. It's a good guess, anyway." He tapped a finger against the page. "It all makes sense if you look at the numbers as dates and times. And it's better than anything else we've come up with."

Gisella once again referred to the book, then back to the location of the graves. Excitement hummed in her. "Actually, I think you said something about these numbers being dates back when we first met and were going through this. Remember?"

"Vaguely."

"Okay, here's my next idea. Look at the map.

All three sets of initials are right here." Her finger jabbed the wall. "RP, JZ, QV. All graves."

Brock leaned closer. "They almost form a triangle, don't they?"

"That's where we need to be before 11:00 tonight."

"Once again, I think you're right." His eyes shone with admiration for her and she ordered herself not to blush.

"Let's go catch us some drug runners."

"I'll contact Border Patrol and tell them to be ready to send backup. We'll need their helicopter with the spotlight."

He pulled out his phone and jumped when Gisella reached out and snagged his hand.

"Wait." She bit her lip. This was all a hunch. What if she was wrong? "Let's just do a little investigating before we call in the big guys. If I'm wrong…"

"It could be embarrassing?"

"To say the least."

"Okay, let's take a drive out there. Do a little snooping around. If we think we're on to something, we'll contact Border Patrol and let them take over."

Relief settled in her. "Perfect. I'll text Levi McDonnell and let him know we're making progress and what our plans are."

Gisella followed Brock back into the waiting area

where they found Krista watching the news. Already, a reporter from El Paso was on the scene at the Boot Hill sheriff's office. The small town was the topic of the evening. Gisella glanced at her watch. Already it was 10:00.

Time to get moving.

"Krista, are you ready?"

"Sure." The teen jumped up from the couch and flipped the television off. She shook her head. "It seems like every time I turn around, the sheriff and Border Patrol are arresting illegals but the news doesn't usually make a big deal out of it like this." She shrugged. "Must have been a particularly large group of them this time."

Gisella cocked her head. "So this happens on a regular basis?"

"Sure. I mean, we are right on the border, you know?"

Gisella frowned. "Yeah. I know."

She shook her head and nodded toward the door. Krista came out last, turned around and locked up. Pocketing the keys, she slid into the car and Brock drove them back to the diner.

Before the girl climbed out, Gisella reached back to squeeze her hand. "Thanks so much for your help."

With a nod and a flash of her pearly whites, Krista

hurried back into the diner to help her Pop finish closing up.

Gisella glanced at her watch again. 10:12. "We have—"

Brock leaned over and placed a kiss on her lips and she froze as his hand came up to cup the back of her neck. But she didn't pull away. When he did, he said, "I don't want the end of this case to be the end of us."

In shock, she couldn't find her voice. She simply stared at him, lips tingling, heart thumping. "Brock…"

"I know we don't have time to get into a discussion right now, but just know that while I have my issues when it comes to you and your job, I still… Just tell me I haven't blown it with you and the possibility of an…us."

Clearing her throat, she nodded. "It's okay. You're right, this isn't the time. We'll talk later, all right?"

Relief stood out on his features. "Good."

"Now, the clock's ticking. Can we go?"

He cranked the car and backed out of the parking lot. Turning right onto the road that would lead to the cemetery, Gisella forced herself to focus on the job at hand. She could think about how much she liked kissing him and the possibility of a permanent relationship with him at a later date.

Hopefully, she'd have some time tomorrow. Because then that would mean this case was over and she'd have the information necessary to arrest the people responsible for Captain Pike's death.

I don't know what's going on with Brock, God, but if he's the one You want me with for the rest of my life, I'm open. Just...protect my heart. And protect us now, please, Lord.

Brock turned into the cemetery and parked near the spot he'd chosen when they'd come to meet Ina. Only this time, she noticed he pulled behind a tighter grove of trees that sheltered the vehicle from the entrance.

Once again, they faced the unknown in the dark of the night. Gisella shivered, not really from the cold, but at the eeriness of it all. After dark in a graveyard. Not exactly her favorite place to be.

But necessary. She'd had to do a lot of unsavory things during her years of law enforcement and she'd learned to just deal.

And she couldn't deny the jolts of excitement that always accompanied an investigation.

With a sideways glance at her partner, she had to admit, she couldn't deny the jolts of excitement she felt around him, either.

The small sliver of the moon made the entire scene before her an unwelcome reminder of when they'd found Ina dead.

She didn't want to find any more bodies. Except live ones that she could arrest.

Brock inclined his head toward the entrance to the cemetery. "I don't think you can see this spot from there."

"Not unless you were looking for it."

"I don't want to advertise our presence here."

She nodded. "Good thinking."

Pulling out the little black book, she pulled out a small penlight; focusing it on the page, she noted the hand-drawn "map." "Now that I know what it is, I can see that it's a smaller replica of the map on the wall of the morgue." She groaned. "Wish I'd figured this out earlier."

"We've got it now. Let's make it work for us."

She smiled at him and let her eyes drink in his rugged good looks. Her heart twisted. She'd become so fond of him. Probably loved him.

And it had happened so fast she hadn't been able to erect and maintain her usual "keep your distance" barriers. He'd barreled his way right through them. And from his earlier actions, she knew he felt the same.

Back to the map, Gisella.

She focused on the drawing, studied it, then looked around. With a nod to her left, she asked, "That way?"

"I think so."

She glanced around one more time, eyes probing the darkness beyond. It was quiet. Almost too quiet.

Another shiver racked her, this time from the cold, and she was grateful for the heavy coat and gloves.

They made their way through the wrought-iron gates, cautious and alert. A sound scraped behind her and Gisella whirled a hand on her gun as Brock palmed his own weapon and they slipped behind a large mausoleum to her right. "What was that?" she whispered.

"I'm not sure," he whispered back. "I don't see anything."

Gisella, positioned behind the large building, felt a flash of déjà vu again. Any moment now, she expected gunshots to break the silence and pound the ground around her. Brock slid close to her, his focus on the area where the sound had come from. Softly, he said, "I brought a flashlight just in case, but I'd hate to use it. I don't want anyone seeing it and coming to investigate yet."

Her eyes caught movement. A shadow to her left. With her gun in her right hand, she reached out to grab Brock's arm and squeezed.

He understood and froze. Her heart pounded. Was someone following them?

Breaths coming in shallow pants as her adrenaline surged, she simply waited.

And heard the faint sound of rustling pebbles. Brock tensed so she knew he heard it, too.

They waited.

And then Brock let out a small laugh. Gisella started. "What is it?"

"Look."

Gisella squinted and finally made out the form of a large dog standing still, eyes glowing in the faint moonlight. A pup hung from her jaws. With a warning growl, she took a step toward them.

Brock backed up and spoke low. "Go on, girl, we're not here for you." Gisella felt Brock's hand clasp hers and pull her back, away from the headstone. She knew he didn't like dogs but admired the fact that he didn't let his fear rule him. She absently wished he'd transfer that over into other parts of his life. Like the one where fear seemed to rule his heart.

Together, they gave the animal her space and she loped off into the trees beyond the entrance.

Gisella pulled in a deep breath, shelved her personal thoughts and holstered her gun. "Now," she said looking back at the book, "where were we?"

"This way."

They made their way to the back of the cemetery. Finally, lights from the border fence filtered through, cutting the darkness better than the moon.

Using her flashlight as a necessary evil, Gisella consulted the picture of the map on her phone, compared it to the map in the book one more time. "Okay, we're almost there."

A moment later, she came to the area they'd been looking for. "X marks the spot."

NINETEEN

Several graves surrounded a large mausoleum. A small cement building, it stood alone. A single light burned at the right edge of the roof, casting an eerie glow on the nearby graves. Wrought-iron bars covered the double cement doors from top to bottom. The right door was cracked. Ignoring the spooky-looking building, Brock moved forward and started examining the letters on the nearest headstones. "Lawrence Polk."

"Nope."

"Rosalinda Pena."

"RP. That could be one of them."

He heard the excitement in her voice and shot her a smile. "Looks like your hunch might be paying off."

He moved to the next one. "Not this one." Then the next and the next until he felt his heart thud with his own excitement. "Quaid Vess."

She moved next to him and breathed, "QV."

Brock hurried to the next one. "Not this one." He moved on.

"It'll make a triangle."

Stopping, he looked at the mausoleum, made a judgment based on the location of the other two graves and said, "Here." He stooped to brush away a tangle of leaves coming from the greenery in the vase perched on top of the headstone. Satisfaction surged. "Jim Zachary."

"JZ. We found them." Her eyes glowed in the dim light.

"But we're not done," he reminded her.

She let out a laugh. "Not by a long shot, but this is what I call progress." Pulling out her phone, she tapped at the keys for a few seconds, then slid it in her back pocket.

Probably letting her fellow Rangers or her boss know what they'd found.

Planting her hands on her hips, she spun in a slow circle. "So, we found it. I totally believe this is a huge breakthrough in the case. But what did we find?" She looked at her watch. He knew she was worried that she was right and at eleven o'clock the bad guys might show up.

Brock studied the layout. The triangle. The mausoleum in the middle. "Look at that page with the map of the cemetery again."

She did and held it angled toward a sliver of light so he could see it. "Okay, there are the three graves.

And look. In the middle. Another set of initials. We haven't found those."

"But that would put them right where the mausoleum is."

She cocked her head. "Then I guess we need to go in there."

"I agree. What time is it?"

"10:40."

"Pretty quiet around here for something to be going down in twenty minutes."

She nodded, disappointment reflected in her gaze. "I agree. Maybe I was wrong about what the eleven meant after all."

Brock placed his hand on the mausoleum door and pulled. It opened without a sound. Gisella stared at it with a raised brow. "Now that's just not right."

"You noticed that, too?"

"Of course. This isn't the most well-kept cemetery. I expected that door to groan and creak like my grandma's joints." She stepped inside then looked back at him. "I can't see a thing. I think the flashlight might be all right to use in here. Necessary, in fact."

He pulled it from his back pocket and handed it to her. "Let me just shut the door before you turn it on."

He didn't think anyone was watching. Then again, he didn't know for sure, so wasn't going to take any chances. Carefully, he pulled the door toward him leaving a finger's-width crack just like he'd found it. "Let me block the crack in the door with my body then you can turn on the light."

"Good idea. Let me know when you're ready."

He shifted his body then said, "Go ahead."

He heard her flip the switch.

Light bathed the tomb and she gasped.

Gisella stared at her eerie surroundings. She was inside a tomb with the door shut. And she was alive. Not exactly how she pictured her interment.

Her heart skipped a beat then pounded faster. Three coffins surrounded her. She wondered where the occupants now spent their eternal days.

Walking to the first coffin, she stared down at it. It was a metal casket that looked like it had been there awhile. A plaque attached to the top of it read, "Lilly Smith. 1929-1999. Beloved wife to Harold Smith."

Gisella swung the flashlight to the second coffin. "Hmm. My guess is that's Harold over there. What do you think?"

Brock's eyes followed the path of her light. "Yep, it's Harold. 1919-1982. Beloved husband to Lilly Smith. Short and simple. I like that. Hey," his voice sharpened, "shine your light over to the left a little, will you?"

She complied. "What is it?" The beam of the light

came into contact with what had caught his interest and she blew out a sharp breath. "Oh."

A skeleton. Scattered along the wall. Empty sockets stared back at her from the skull and even though she didn't spook easily, she couldn't help the shiver that ran through her. Gisella shifted closer and said softly, "Okay, why is this person not where he or she belongs?"

"Good question."

Gieslla ran the light over the skeleton, focusing on the skull. "Hmm. A hole in the temple. This was either murder or suicide," she muttered.

Brock pointed to the third coffin, interrupting her musings. "Look. Does the lid on that one look odd?"

Gisella peered closer. "Yes, now that you mention it."

He moved from the door, pressed his fingertips underneath the edge of it and lifted. It opened without a sound. Just like the door.

Heart thudding, Gisella pointed the light down into the coffin and sucked in a lungful of air. "Brock, do you see what I see?"

"A ladder."

"They pulled that body out of this coffin and turned it into…whatever they turned it into."

She looked at the metal structure that had been bolted into the dirt wall. Then she glanced up at him. "Take a deep breath. Did you notice the air quality in here, too?"

He did as she suggested then nodded. "It's not musty or moldy like it's been closed up."

"Someone is in here on a regular basis."

He peered over the edge. "I think we just found how our drug runners are getting across the border so effectively."

"I think you're right. Are you coming?" Excitement sounded in her voice.

"Wouldn't miss it."

She shot him a grin then swinging a leg over the edge of the coffin, eased herself down onto the first step. She flashed the light in front of her. "Let's see where this goes."

Brock followed close behind her. Gisella aimed the light, first in one direction, then another. A flash of white along the bottom edge of the dirt wall caught her eye.

Swooping in like a bird of prey, she zeroed in on the item. She knelt. "A small package of drugs?" she questioned.

"A lab would have to confirm it, of course, but I'm guessing it's not baby powder. Must have fallen out of someone's bag and he didn't catch it."

Gisella snagged her phone from the clip on her pants. "I think it's time to bring in the cavalry." She punched in Ben's number. He would arrange to send in the authorities from the Border Patrol to set up a watch and see who they could catch coming and going from this place.

Holding the phone between her chin and her shoulder, she shined the light on her watch. 10:56.

Then she realized the phone wasn't ringing. Pulling it away from her ear, she checked the signal strength. Nothing. "Great. No signal. As much as I want to explore this tunnel, I want to call this in more."

Brock nodded and turned to head back the way they came.

Single file, they ascended the steps. Brock climbed out of the coffin and reached down to help her up and out.

Gisella started to shut the coffin lid when a noise caught her attention. Brock reached out and grasped her hand.

He'd heard it, too.

No sooner had she flicked off the flashlight than she felt his gloved finger slide against her lips. She nodded and dislodged his finger. He made little noise as he moved and the sliver of light coming from the crack in the door disappeared. But she could picture him pressing his ear to the opening.

Voices reached her. Clear voices. Near voices. And she didn't need her ear pressed up against the crack to hear them. "I'm telling you," one said, "they'll be here within a minute."

"They better have the money. I'm not playing games."

"They'll have it. Quit your whining."

Brock whirled from the door and grasped her arm. Leaning down, he whispered in her ear, "They're headed this way and we've got no backup. Let's head back down the tunnel and see if we learn any more. If they keep talking, they may reveal something that will lead us to a bigger slice of the pie."

Gisella didn't hesitate. She moved back to the coffin and climbed in. Brock followed and pulled the lid shut this time.

Pitch black greeted her eyes once more but she didn't dare use the flashlight in case someone opened the lid to look down into the tunnel.

She felt him touch her arm, then his hand slid down to wrap her gloved fingers in his. "If we have to move," he whispered, "I don't want us to get separated."

She squeezed his hand and waited, listening, frustrated with herself and the fact that she hadn't contacted someone before heading down into the tunnel. But there hadn't been time. They'd barely made it down as it was.

Boots thumped against the floor overhead. Gisella stepped down the steps as silently as possible. She didn't want to be visible if they opened the lid.

Brock stepped after her and she had no doubt he shared her concern. At the bottom, she stopped, turned and waited.

From above, a beacon of light appeared. Brock pulled her blindly back into the tunnel. "They've opened the lid," she whispered.

"If they decide to come down, we're going to have to use the tunnel or face them."

And then light from the other end bounced off the wall in front of Gisella and she sucked in a breath. "Or we can figure out how to not be caught in the middle."

TWENTY

Brock's mind raced. Bad guys behind them and more in front of them. Brock's thoughts worked through and discarded one plan after another at the speed of light.

He could hear them getting closer. The tunnel lightened due to a very bright light the approaching group carried. Gisella squeezed his hand and pulled him toward the bouncing light. "What are you doing?" he whispered.

"Trust me."

His gloved fingers wrapped around his weapon. The other gripped Gisella's hand. He let her lead.

The light ahead grew brighter.

The voices louder.

She turned a corner with a sudden move and pulled him behind her. Once again they were bathed in darkness, the part of the tunnel they'd just come from now lit up like the sun. As long as no one pointed the light in this direction, the men would walk right past them.

A mixture of Spanish and English reached him. They were talking about the drugs. Anger gripped him around the throat. They discussed it openly, no fear or anxiety in their voices. Instead, it sounded like their weekly conversation about their most recent entertainment.

Laughter ricocheted off the walls and his gut tightened even more.

Leaning down, he whispered against her ear while breathing in her unique scent. "How many voices do you count?"

"Five, maybe six. Could be more though, and they're just not joining in the fun." Her voice was barely there. A quiet mist on a winter morning.

Real fear filled him at the thought of her falling into these men's hands. His heart shuddered at the thought. Somehow, he would get her out of this.

The light passed them as well as the shuffling sound of booted feet. Their shadows were briefly illuminated on the far wall and he saw that each man carried a load on his back.

Backpacks full of drugs most likely. Anger stirred. He wanted these men put away. Part of him wanted to rush out there, gun blazing. But he restrained himself.

Be patient, these are the peons. Let them lead you to the big guys.

As the light faded, Brock's breathing slowed.

Then Gisella pulled at his hand once more. She

led the way from their hiding place, her fingers trailing the wall like a blind person, back out into the main tunnel. She turned right and Brock listened to the men's receding footsteps. "Why do you seem to know where you're going?"

"It's the picture from the book." Once again he had to strain to hear her. Which was good. That meant whoever else was down there wouldn't hear her, either. "The drawing that we thought were roads. It occurred to me it might be the tunnel. When we were about to be caught in the middle, I realized I had to take a chance. Fortunately, it paid off."

"You're amazing."

"Shh."

She'd turned and twisted a couple of times and Brock realized he had no idea where he was. But Gisella didn't seem to have the same problem. "Now—" she leaned close "—if I've remembered correctly, we've come full circle and this is going to take us back to the steps. If they're gone, we can go up and slip out. If they're not…"

"…we'll wait them out."

"Right."

Together, single file, they made their way back to the main tunnel and finally the steps. Brock didn't know how she knew where she was going in the inky blackness, but he followed her lead and trailed his fingers against the wall.

When she came to the end, he was relieved to

realize no light reached his eyes. Which meant the bad guys were up above.

Gisella flicked the flashlight on and a faint glow surrounded them. She'd covered it with her hand to avoid its full power. Brock saw the stairs just in front of him. "Let me go first."

If someone heard them, or opened the coffin lid unexpectedly, at least he would be in front of Gisella if that someone had a weapon.

Ignoring the stubborn thrust of her jaw that said she wanted to argue with him, he stepped ahead of her and started climbing.

Gisella grasped the rung to close in on Brock.

A footstep sounded behind her and she whirled, one hand on the rung, the other reaching for her weapon.

A light flashed in her eyes blinding her, but not before she saw a glint bounce off a gun held steadily in a brown hand.

"Brock! He's got a gun!" The words ripped from her even as instinct compelled her sideways and onto the dirt floor.

The man lunged forward and Gisella dodged his swinging hand. If he fired the weapon in the confined space, they'd all be deaf if not dead from a possible cave-in.

Brock landed beside her with a grunt. The light moved closer. Gisella didn't hesitate as she scrambled to her feet and kicked out. Their attacker screamed and the light skittered across the dirt, bouncing shadows from one wall to the other.

Satisfaction curled inside her as she realized her judgment was good and she'd connected with flesh and bone. Then dismay as she swallowed the fact that she'd kicked the wrong hand. She'd been aiming for the gun. Vaguely she wondered about the men above and prayed they were far enough in the tunnel that their struggles were muffled.

Thankfully, the man still hadn't fired the weapon.

But that didn't mean he wouldn't when he had a good shot.

Determined not to give him one, she moved left.

Brock jumped out from beside her and clipped the man around the knees.

The two crashed to the dirt floor. Gisella scrambled for the light. Snatching it up, she turned it on the struggling duo. Brock caught a punch to the eye and reared back. But before the attacker could gather the strength for another blow, Brock's fist landed on the man's jaw.

And he went still.

Panting, Brock rolled away from the now-stunned smuggler. Gisella kicked the gun against the dirt wall and slapped the first cuff on the man's thick wrist.

Brock shoved him onto his stomach and finished the job.

"Are you all right?" she asked.

"Yeah. I'll have a shiner and probably a headache, but yeah, I'm good. You?"

"Peachy." She looked around. "No one's coming down here. I guess we're still undetected for now."

Brock grunted. "What do you want to do with him?"

"Tie your bandanna around his mouth and let's handcuff him somewhere back in one of the side areas."

"Works for me." Brock whipped the bandanna from around his neck and fashioned a gag for their prisoner. Gisella took the cuffs Brock held out to her and fitted the first one around the chain connecting the ones attached to the man's wrist. As Brock forced the man to walk, she found a rung attached to the wall, probably used by the smugglers to find their way in the dark. She snapped the second cuff around this. Then she grabbed the gun she'd kicked against the wall and stuck it into her waistband in the small of her back.

It wasn't comfortable, but would have to do because she sure wasn't leaving it with the prisoner.

Brock walked to the ladder, placed his foot on the first rung and began climbing.

Gisella quickly followed and soon, he was at the top.

Once there, he closed his eyes and listened.

Nothing. Had the men stepped outside of the tomb to conduct their business? They would have had to or he would have heard voices. And they would have already put in an appearance to see what was going on below. Were they even still there?

Surely they were or he and Gisella would have been trapped once again in the tunnel with the bad guys bearing down on them.

With a cautious push, he lifted the lid of the coffin an inch. More darkness. He felt Gisella behind him on the steps, impatience radiating from her. Yet she remained silent and let him take the lead.

Another push and the lid lifted a few more inches. Still no light. No one was in the tomb. He finished opening it, reached in and grasped her hand. "Come on. We're good." Keeping his voice low, he said, "They've gone outside. Let's get out if we can, but be on your guard. As soon as they realize our friend back there is missing, they might come looking for him."

Brock pictured the door in relation to the coffin and moved toward it, hands outstretched. When his fingertips touched it, he slid them down to find the knob. It occurred to him that someone must have added that when they'd decided to build the tunnel.

Why would a mausoleum need a knob on the inside?

Turning it slowly, he inched the door open, not

worried about it making any noise, but more worried about the location of the men. He didn't like not being able to see what he was walking into.

Once he had the door open enough to look out, he saw lights in the distance. A car had parked opposite the mausoleum and the men were gathered around it. He placed a call to the sheriff and requested backup keeping his voice in a low whisper. No one looked his way.

"Backup should be on the way," he whispered back to Gisella then nodded in the direction of the men. "They're distracted for now. I'm going to see if I can get a little closer and hear what they're saying."

"I'm right behind you."

Brock grimaced at her statement. He'd hoped she would stay behind, but he had to admit he wasn't surprised at her insistence on going with him. Not that he thought she couldn't handle herself, but it sure would make him feel better knowing she was tucked away somewhere safe.

He started toward the men, ducking behind tombstones just as he'd done when he'd been avoiding gunfire only a couple of days before.

Fortunately for Brock and Gisella, the car's headlights illuminated the area in front of it, leaving the surrounding area still dark so that if someone looked in their direction, they would still be protected by the night.

But the men didn't seem too worried about being caught as they never took their attention from whoever was in the car issuing orders. And handing out cash.

An arm shot out of the window and handed a handful of money to each man, one by one. As the men received their money, they repositioned their now-empty backpacks over their shoulders.

"Hey! Paco! Where are you?" The one who'd just received his money called out in Spanish and looked around.

Brock sped up.

Gisella glided behind him on silent feet, her weapon held ready in her right hand.

They reached a large tombstone and ducked behind it. Peering around the edge, Brock saw one of the men move.

He headed that way and as he moved, Brock caught a glimpse of two men in the car. One was just a shadow that he couldn't make out, but the light from one of the smuggler's flashlights illuminated a face he knew well.

Niles Vernon.

TWENTY-ONE

Gisella's stomach burned as she honed in on the agent.

A dirty cop. She didn't want to believe it, but she couldn't deny the evidence right before her eyes. Disgust curled inside her and she gripped her gun, ready to come out and arrest them all by herself.

But that would be stupid.

The one who'd called out for Paco—probably the guy in the tunnel—walked toward the mausoleum. Gisella saw that Brock had his weapon trained on the man.

Snatching her phone, she punched in a text to the sheriff asking for backup, then one to Levi letting him know what was going on.

He would call in the reinforcements. Without waiting for confirmation that he'd received the text, she tucked the phone back on her clip and got ready to go on the defensive with the man looking for Paco.

Brock waited until she nodded at him to let him know that backup was on the way. An angry shout made her duck and her heartbeat jerk into overdrive. Had they been discovered?

A gun cracked, a man screamed. Gisella peered around the edge of the tombstone to see a body on the ground in front of the car. The one who'd been headed their way spun on his heel to watch everything play out.

Niles stood behind the open driver's door, his gun held casually in his hand. His eyes scanned the now-silent group of eight men. "Anyone else think I'm cheating them?"

No one responded and Niles smirked. "Yeah. That's what I thought. You have your orders. Don't mess up." He gave a casual wave to the man he'd shot. "And clean that up. Take him back with you. I don't need any evidence he was here."

Everything in Gisella wanted to confront the murderous Border Patrol agent, but these men were all armed, all dangerous—and all scared of Niles Vernon.

It would be suicide for her and Brock to reveal themselves without help.

Headlights illuminated the area in front of her and Gisella breathed a prayer that it was backup. The group froze at the approach of the vehicle then scattered when they saw it was a patrol car. Niles swore and thumped a hand on the hood of his car, but didn't run.

Probably thought he could handle the sheriff,

Gisella decided. She looked over at Brock and saw him watching, waiting for just the right moment.

Satisfaction thumped in her. Niles didn't know she and Brock were the ones that had called in the re-inforcements. Then she frowned at the single patrol car. Where were the rest of them? Surely, the sheriff didn't think he could take care of this alone?

Then again, he was probably counting on her and Brock to help him out.

Still…

The car rolled to a stop and the sheriff got out of the driver's side. Chris Locke climbed from the passenger seat.

Sheriff Johnston's booming voice cut through the sudden silence. "What's the problem, Vernon?"

"What do you want, Kip? There's no problem. I told you I could handle this."

"You can, huh? Why aren't you answering your radio? And where's the Ranger and her sidekick? We've got company downtown. Two more Rangers."

Gisella saw Brock frown at the slight insult. She kept her focus on the men before her even while her eyes scanned the surrounding area. Two more Rangers? Levi and Evan? Ben had sent help even though she'd told him she didn't need it. Instead of feeling insulted, she was grateful. She just hoped Levi had gotten her text about her current location. She'd sent that text just as an FYI. Now, she realized it might very well bring the Rangers to her and Brock's aid.

Maybe.

The smugglers from Juarez had scattered, but no doubt they hadn't gone far, hoping Niles would deal with the sheriff and they could conclude their business.

Niles shrugged. "How would I know? I had business to take care of tonight and it didn't include babysitting." He moved to climb back into his vehicle, resting his hand on top of the open door. "Guess you scared my business off."

The sheriff scowled. "I got a call that they were here and requesting backup."

At that, Niles jerked. "Here? Where?"

Gisella and Brock exchanged a glance. She whispered, "If we let him drive off, he'll get rid of the drugs in the car and we'll lose our evidence. We can't wait any longer."

"I agree. I'd feel better with more help, but you're right."

"I'll help the sheriff and Chris arrest Niles. You watch for anyone who decides to come back and fight." He nodded and she stepped from behind the stone to point her weapon at Niles.

"Freeze, Niles! You're under arrest."

Niles did as ordered and froze. More in shock than in any desire to follow her command. He rotated, hands held where she could see them and met her gaze.

His wary eyes narrowed. "For what?"

"Smuggling drugs. I think we're going to find something real interesting in the contents of those backpacks that you threw in the back of your car. Sheriff, Locke." She glanced at the two men. "I need a set of cuffs, please. I had to leave mine down in the tunnel."

"What tunnel?" Chris demanded.

"Long story," Brock murmured from behind her. He kept his back to her back and she knew he was watching for any threatening movement, determined not to be taken by surprise by a returning smuggler.

The sheriff held up a hand. "Hold on a second." He glared at Gisella. "Why would you want to arrest Agent Vernon? Are you out of your mind?"

"Hardly." She gave a ten-second explanation of what she and Brock witnessed. "The men who brought the drugs over from Juarez are still in the woods somewhere."

The sheriff's face turned red in the light of the headlights. He said to Niles, "You really messed up this time, Vernon."

Niles ignored the sheriff and smirked at her. "I'm afraid you're mistaken, Ranger. I'm not going anywhere."

Not for the first time that night, Gisella developed

a bad feeling in her gut. But she wasn't here to debate the issue with him. "Pull your weapon out of the holster and give it to the sheriff."

The sheriff pulled his gun and pointed it at the Border Patrol agent.

Then swung it around on Gisella and Brock. "Actually, Ranger, why don't you and your partner drop your weapons?"

Brock froze. Then, gun held out to his side in a non-threatening manner, swung around to face the sheriff, Niles and Chris. All three had their weapons trained on him and Gisella.

"Well," Brock muttered, "that explains a lot."

"So, you're the ones who didn't want us here."

Gisella's words came out flat, a statement of fact loaded with disgust. Her lip curled and she still held on to her gun, finger twitching near the trigger.

The sheriff's "good ol' country boy" persona disappeared as his eyes took on the consistency of chipped ice. "Don't be stupid, Ranger. You might get off a shot, but you and your partner will be dead before you can blink."

Gisella gave a low sound in her throat then slowly lowered her gun to the ground at her feet.

"Kick it," the sheriff ordered.

Brock tossed his and Gisella gave hers a swipe with her right foot.

Sheriff Johnston motioned for Niles to get the

weapons. The man did so while Chris kept his gun trained on them.

On Brock.

Brock sneered, "That area of the fence on the border, it was all set up for us, wasn't it? Something to throw us off if we came snooping?"

Niles grinned. "Worked, too, didn't it?" Keeping his gun on Gisella, he yelled in the direction of the trees, "Get out here!"

As though he'd waved a wand, the eight men from the tunnel started appearing from behind headstones and from the trees bordering the cemetery. Hard dark eyes stared at them.

The sheriff motioned for the men to disappear back down the tunnel. "Get on back where you belong."

Like disturbed ants, they scuttled toward the mausoleum door and disappeared. No doubt the man who'd surprised them in the tunnel would be gone by the time he and Gisella got out of this.

If they got out of it.

Brock's nerves of steel seemed to have deserted him in the face of Gisella's danger. He wasn't worried so much about himself, but Gisella…

He shuddered. "What happened to Jasper West? I'm guessing he didn't just escape. Billings helped you set it up to look like he did while in actuality, he's probably dead. How am I doing so far?"

The sheriff scowled. "Shut up."

"So what happened to him?" Brock asked.

The sheriff's lips twitched. "Let's just say Jasper was expendable. More trouble than he was worth. Just like you two."

So Jasper was dead. Brock hated the loss of life, but the man had made the choices that had led to his end. "You're the one who made sure the medical examiner didn't have a chance to gather the evidence on Ina, aren't you?"

With an exasperated sigh, the sheriff said, "Of course. Now enough." He looked at Chris and Niles. "Kill 'em, then get rid of the evidence."

Chris told the sheriff, "I'll take care of it." He gave a cruel smile. "It'll be my pleasure."

Brock's palms started to sweat. Gisella hadn't moved so much as a muscle in the last couple of minutes, but her eyes weren't still and he could almost hear her brain thinking.

"Look…" He held out a hand and Chris's finger curled around the trigger. "If you thought we were trouble before, you have no idea the mess you'll create for yourself if you kill us. Plus, we've got backup on the way." Uneasily, he realized a lot of time had passed. Backup should be here by now.

The sheriff barked a laugh. "Not hardly. I got the message from my dispatcher and told her I'd handle it. I took care of your backup." He looked at Chris. "Now do it."

Chris lifted a brow. "Here? I don't think so. Get

some cuffs on them and throw them in the trunk of your car. I'll send them to the bottom of the lake and we'll be done with them. No bodies, no blood, nothing to explain."

The sheriff hesitated then narrowed his eyes. "No. Do it right here, right now."

Chris shrugged. "Whatever." He lifted the gun and pointed it at Gisella.

Brock saw her brace herself even as his muscles tightened in readiness to lunge—at the man or in front of Gisella, whichever would save her life.

Then Chris whipped the gun toward Niles and fired. Niles hit the ground with a yell. Brock didn't allow himself to wonder or feel surprise at the sudden reprieve. From the corner of his eye, he saw Gisella dive for cover even as Brock threw himself toward the Border Patrol agent who'd dropped his gun.

Brock's own weapon was too far away to attempt to retrieve, and he wouldn't have time to go for his weapon at his ankle before Niles had his own weapon back in hand.

Brock landed next to Niles as the man's fingers grazed the barrel of the gun.

"Freeze! Texas Rangers! Put down your weapons!"

Levi. He'd gotten her text and must have acted immediately to get here so fast. Gisella heard his shouted command even as she watched the sheriff level his gun on her.

She had no weapon and no time to grab the one she'd been forced to toss. As though in slow motion, from the corner of her eye, she saw Brock's gun rise and take aim at the sheriff.

The guns fired.

Gisella launched herself behind the nearest headstone.

Something slammed into the side of her head and blackness blanketed her.

TWENTY-TWO

Brock saw the sheriff stumble against the car then fall to the ground. Desperately, he scanned the area where Gisella had been.

Nothing.

A helicopter thumped overhead. Lights from it swept the area, illuminating it well. Siren screams rent the night and law enforcement descended. Brock saw the El Paso logo on the cruisers.

He stumbled to the fallen sheriff and swept his gun aside. A tall, blond man with a badge pinned to his shirt—a badge that looked just like Gisella's—helped a whining yet belligerent Niles Vernon to his feet. "I need a doctor before I bleed out."

"You'll live." The Ranger snapped cuffs on the man then said, "Hey, Evan, you see Gisella anywhere?"

The Asian Ranger looked around and frowned. "No."

Brock's worry alarm went on high alert. "Gisella?"

No answer.

Brock picked through the sea of faces now swarming the area. But didn't see the one he most wanted to see.

Where was she? He thought back to the scene. His last mental picture of her was when she'd dived behind the tombstone to his left.

Leaving the wounded sheriff in the capable hands of the nearest Ranger, Brock searched for Gisella while his heart threatened to thump out of his chest. Two ambulances arrived, he noted absently as he rounded the next large tombstone.

And came to a panicked halt. "Gisella!" She lay on her side. The helicopter still pounded above him. Someone shouted an order from behind him. But nothing registered except the fact that the woman he loved lay before him.

Brock bolted to her side and knelt. Terrified, he reached for a pulse and relaxed only slightly when he felt it beat softly against his fingers.

He rolled her onto her back and saw the blood on her forehead. "Hey!" he yelled. "Over here!"

Rushing feet vibrated the earth beneath him. "What is it?"

Brock looked up into the eyes of the man that could only be Levi McDonnell. "Get a paramedic. She's hurt."

It was only then that he noticed the blood seeping from the hole in her pants.

She'd been shot.

In the head and the leg? His heart ached at the sight and he wanted to grab his weapon and empty it into the men who'd done this to her.

But he couldn't. All he could do was hold her hand and pray for help. *God, she needs you. And I need her. You put her in my life for a reason. I believe that now. Don't let her die on me.* Then words failed him as he clung to the woman who had shown him the way back to his faith and the God who'd never given up on him.

Gisella thought her head might rupture if it pounded any harder. And then there was the pain in her right leg. A shooting pain that traveled up into her hip and along her back.

What had she done to herself?

Biting back a groan, she opened her eyes, squinting in the dark room.

Where was she? What had happened? She closed her eyes once again and forced her brain to think.

Oh, yeah. She'd been shot. And she'd taken a nosedive into a headstone in her effort to get out of the way of the bullet the sheriff had meant for her.

The bullet that had been surgically removed from her leg yesterday. Or was that two days ago?

A warm hand wrapped around hers and she jumped. "Who…"

The smell of vanilla registered and she knew exactly who sat at her side.

"Mom?"

"Hi, baby."

"Oh, boy." She sucked in a ragged breath and felt tears sting her eyes. "I bet you're furious with me, aren't you?"

Her mother didn't speak. Probably gathering her thoughts.

Gisella wanted to sink back into oblivion. Even that was better than the lecture she knew was coming. "Mom, I'm not in the mood for…" She stopped. "Well, you know."

Still her mother remained quiet.

Where was her dad?

"Your father decided we needed some time alone so as soon as he knew you were going to be all right, he went to get some coffee."

Oh, boy. She heard her mother pull in a breath. *Here it comes.*

"Te amo, mija."

Gisella froze. "What?"

"I love you, my daughter." Her mother's Mexican accent grew thick. "I love you more than you will ever understand. That is, until you have a child of your own."

"I…um…love you, too, Mom." Gisella still didn't relax. Where was the woman going with this?

"I've missed you," her mother whispered.

Gisella felt the tears close in. "I know, Mom, I've missed you, too."

"And I owe you an apology."

Who was this woman and what had happened to her mother? Gisella was too stunned to speak.

As though reading Gisella's thoughts, her mother gave a sad smile. "I've been a foolish old woman and only realized that my fear of losing you was causing that very thing to happen."

Gisella thought about the phone calls she'd ignored, the excuses she'd made for missing holiday meals, the work she'd buried herself in.

Her mother wasn't the only one who needed to apologize. "I'm sorry."

"It's okay, darling, you go back to sleep. We'll talk more when you're better."

Gisella wanted to go back to sleep, to close her eyes and sink back into the comfort of dark nothingness. "Brock," she whispered. "I want to see Brock."

Where was he?

In the lobby of the hospital, Brock paced, trying to decide what to do. He didn't want to lose Gisella and yet he didn't want to wind up like his partner, either. Gisella could have been killed. Had almost been killed more than once in the last week.

He'd struggled with whether he could live with that on a daily basis. Then again, he struggled with whether he could live without her.

Would he love her any less if they were apart?

Would he think about her any less if he didn't see her every day?

No. To both questions.

His heart wavered.

Lord, You placed her in my life. She led me back to You. Then You gave me the unique opportunity to get to know her and fall in love with her. Would I be wrong to give that up? Would I be throwing it all back in Your face by refusing to get over my fear of losing her?

"She's awake."

Brock turned. Levi stood there with a woman who looked so much like Gisella, he knew immediately this was Gisella's mother. He strode to her and took her hand in his. "I'm Brock."

She gave him a gentle smile. "I know. She's asking for you."

He nodded. "Thanks."

Pulling in a deep breath, he strode toward the elevator.

Gisella appreciated everyone coming to see her, but she couldn't seem to lift herself out of the depression that had settled over her. She was thrilled that she and her parents had made their peace, but the one person she needed to talk to hadn't shown his face.

She clicked the television off and grimaced. At

least the awful headache had faded and the pain in her leg dulled to manageable.

A knock on the door made her jump. "Come in."

And there he was. The man she wanted to see. "Brock," she breathed. Then cleared her throat. *Don't act like a lovesick idiot.*

She'd just given her report to Ben and Levi had left with her mother. The flowers gracing the room attested to the fact that she was loved by those who knew her.

And while she didn't take that lightly, right now she was only interested in the love of one person.

He walked toward her and her breath caught in her throat. It shocked her how much she'd come to care for this man in such a short time. They'd experienced things that had brought them close extremely fast. She admired him, respected him...loved him.

But how did he feel?

"How are you doing?"

"I'm scared."

That caught him by surprise. "What do you mean?"

She blinked. "I'm not sure. It just kind of popped out." She licked her lips and shifted as she processed what she'd said. "I guess I'm scared you're going to tell me goodbye and we'll never have a chance to figure out what's between us." She flushed and looked away. "I don't even know if that makes sense."

He cupped her chin. "It makes sense." Leaning

down, he placed a kiss on her lips—a lingering, exploring, questioning kiss.

Gisella thought her heart might just explode. When he pulled back, she studied his eyes. "Does this mean you're not saying goodbye?"

"There are no goodbyes in our future, Gisella. At least not until God is ready for us to part ways."

Gladness, joy and hope filled her, rushing together, mingling inside of her until she wasn't sure what she was feeling.

She just knew she felt good for the first time in two days.

Another knock on the door sounded. "Come in."

Chris Locke entered and Gisella lifted her brows in surprise. She'd wondered what had happened to the man after the showdown in the cemetery. She'd been grateful to the man who'd probably been instrumental in saving their lives, but hadn't heard what had happened to him since.

When he flashed his badge, she gasped. "You were undercover?"

"Yeah. I'm DEA from Oklahoma. My boss and yours have been watching the town of Boot Hill for a while. They decided to join forces and send me undercover." He shoved his hands in his pockets. "Sorry I was such a jerk to you guys, but that was the character I was playing so I had to keep up appearances."

Brock shook his head. "I didn't even suspect. I even had you checked out."

Chris offered a wry grin. "I figured you would. I called my boss shortly after meeting you that first night in the restaurant and warned him to make sure my cover was so solid not even a fellow agent would be able to uncover it."

"He did a good job," Brock grunted.

Chris gazed back at Gisella. "And you two did a great job of finding the tunnel. We figured there was one somewhere, but the sheriff and Niles never let me in on the location. Anyway, we're all grateful that one more piece of that drug-running operation has been stopped."

"Thanks."

"Well, I won't stay." He placed his hand on the door. "I just wanted to stop by and say that I hope we can work together again in the future sometime."

Brock nodded. "You bet."

The door shut behind the man and Gisella leaned her head back against the pillow. "God sure works in mysterious ways, doesn't He?"

Brock smiled. "He sure does. Now, where were we?"

She flushed. "I think you were telling me that there weren't going to be any goodbyes in our future and that—"

Another knock on the door interrupted her.

Brock grimaced and Gisella gave an exasperated sigh then called, "Come in."

The door swung open once again and this time her captain, Ben Fritz, stepped through. Gisella swallowed and straightened her shoulders. She'd been told he'd stopped by just to visit earlier, but she'd been out of it.

"Hi, Ben."

A relieved smile crossed his handsome face. "Hey, Gisella. You're looking a lot better than the last time I saw you."

"I feel better." She gestured toward Brock. "Have the two of you met?"

Brock nodded. "In the waiting room." The two men shook hands.

Ben stepped to the edge of her bed and looked down at her. "I thought I'd stop by and fill you in. When does the doctor think you'll be out of here?"

"Tomorrow at the latest, why?"

"With your wounded leg, you can't be back in the field until you're healed, but we can get you back to San Antonio and assign you to Quin Morton's room. We need someone to watch him, protect him if there's trouble. And let us know the minute he recovers enough to talk."

Gisella grimaced. Boring. But necessary. "Sure, that sounds like a good plan."

"Good." He removed his hat and ran his hands

through his hair. "We've had some good interrogation sessions with Johnston and Vernon. They couldn't wait to turn on each other and squeal about everything they know. And the combination of numbers and letters in the little black book were the longitude and latitude for the mausoleum."

Gisella groaned and shook her head gently. "I should have seen it."

"You didn't need it. You figured it out without that bit of information. We also got the location of a warehouse about a mile from the cemetery where they were stashing the drugs. Apparently, Niles would meet the men at the tunnel, get the backpacks full of drugs and drop them at the warehouse."

A knock on the door made her laugh. Brock joined in. Ben looked a little confused at their laughter. She'd explain later.

"Come in," Gisella called.

Levi McDonnell entered carrying a huge bouquet of flowers. He flashed his charming grin at her. "Where do you want these?"

Brock stood and took them from the Ranger. "I think the only space available is on top of the television."

Levi crossed his arms over his chest. "Glad to see you're feeling better, Gisella. You've had a lot of people worried about you."

"No kidding," Brock muttered. Gisella heard him and flashed him a sweet smile.

Turning her attention to Levi, she said, "Fill me in, will you? I don't think Ben's gotten around to telling me everything."

Running a rough hand down a cheek, Levi gathered his thoughts then said, "The threatening letters about the Alamo anniversary celebration have stopped and we're still trying to figure out why. The sheriff and Niles are still talking like they're in a competition to see who can get the best deal and the lightest sentence. They both say something big is about to happen in March, but they don't know what." He gave a growl of frustration. "And they still insist that Jorge Cantana and Axle Hudson were their only contacts and they don't know anyone in the organization further up than that."

Gisella grimaced. "That doesn't help us one bit. Jorge still won't say a word because he's afraid for his family and Axle can't talk because he's dead."

Ben nodded. "One interesting thing is that Mr. Morton's just started gesturing to the Alamo picture on the wall in his hospital room. We've concluded that with his gesturing and his knowledge of the Lions' plans that there's a connection between the threats and the Alamo celebration planned in March."

"And," Levi offered, "in an attempt to find out what that is, I'm going to become the inside man. I've been assigned to work on-site at the Alamo over the next several weeks. While there, I'll be doing a lot of digging to see what I can come up with and what the best route is to keep the officials at the ceremony safe."

Gisella nodded. "That sounds like an excellent plan."

Ben grasped her hand. "As soon as they let you out of here and you've recovered as much as you need to, I need you back in San Antonio on Quin."

"I'll be there," she promised.

The frown on Brock's face didn't encourage her, but she knew they were on the way to figuring out their relationship so she didn't let it worry her too much.

"What about Jasper West and the hotel clerk, Steve Billings?"

Ben said, "Jasper was found dead. Dumped in the lake. He just surfaced this morning. It was an execution style with a single bullet to the head."

"Ugh." Gisella grimaced.

"And Steve?" Brock pressed.

"Still alive and kicking." Ben rubbed a hand over his mouth. "We don't think he's connected to the Lions other than he was willing to kill for money. He served time for a homicide from six years ago. Hit and run. Got out of prison two years ago. Honestly, he seemed like he was on the straight and narrow until the sheriff talked him into helping get rid of you two. He figured it would be easy money and he had the sheriff on his side if anything happened."

Brock grunted. "Guess he didn't count on the sheriff being arrested."

"No, he definitely didn't count on that." Ben slapped his thigh and said, "I guess that about covers it. You need to rest."

Ben and Levi left with promises to check up on her.

Gisella looked at Brock. Arms crossed over his chest and face set in a scowl, she sighed and said, "Okay, spill it."

The scowl faded and he stepped closer to sit on the bed beside her. His hand reached out to touch the white bandage wrapped around her head.

Then his fingers trailed over the wound on her blanket-covered leg. "I could have lost you." His rough, low words hurt her heart. She heard the pain in his voice and knew he was thinking of his partner. The one who'd lost the woman he'd loved.

"But you didn't."

Brock loved her. She knew he did. But did he love her enough? Enough to defeat the fear she could see coursing through him? Enough to banish the past and press on toward the future? Their future?

His eyes met hers and she bit her lip. He finally sighed and leaned forward to rest his forehead gently against hers. "You have to finish this, don't you?"

"We still don't know who killed Gregory Pike. I don't think any of us that were in his Company can rest until we find the killer."

"I understand. If I were in your shoes, I'd feel the same way. I don't like it, but I do understand."

"I know you do," she whispered. "It's one of the things I love about you."

He froze at the word "love."

Gisella decided to throw caution to the wind. "I know it's been fast. It seems impossible to fall in love with someone in only a week and have it last, but it's happened to me." She looked away from him and stared out of the window across the room. "I'm spilling my heart here, Brock. I really need to know how you feel because if you're going to walk away from me, I need to shut up now."

For a long moment he didn't move and Gisella felt her breath clog in her throat. Had she said too much? Been too blunt?

His weight shifted beside her and then his soft voice reached her ears. "Aw, Gisella. I've already told you there aren't any goodbyes in our future. You're amazing, you know that?"

Feeling the heat in her cheeks and sliver of fear in her heart, she muttered, "Thanks. But?"

"No but. I had a long talk with God."

Her brow lifted. "You did? What did you talk about?"

"Mostly you. And my old partner. And fear. And choices in life."

"Heavy topics." She kept her voice light. Where was he going with this? Her head began to throb.

"Yes, very heavy. But…" He smiled. "It seems I've managed to get past my fear of developing a relationship with someone I work with."

Gisella couldn't help the small chuckle that escaped her. She winced at the pain that shot through her head. "Yeah. Looks like."

"It won't be easy," he said, his words soft, intense.

"Most things worth fighting for don't come easy." Like her job and being on the path to repairing the relationship with her parents.

And loving Brock.

"True." He paused. "I can't promise I won't worry about you."

Her heart lifted. "Same here. Your job isn't exactly the safest on the planet, you know. And you take unnecessary chances sometimes." She frowned. "If anyone should be thinking twice about a relationship, it's me."

He smiled and nodded even though her joke fell flat. She sighed and reached out with both hands to cup his face. "The Lord is my light and my salvation…whom shall I fear? The Lord is the stronghold of my life…of whom shall I be afraid?"

His eyes flared. "I read that last night," he whispered in awe. "I also chose to trust in Him. I'm giving Him my fear and jumping into loving you with both feet. How does that sound?"

Gisella felt joy erupt in her. She wrapped both

arms around his neck and pulled him close to kiss him lightly. "I think that sounds like the smartest choice you've made in a long time."

* * * * *

Dear Reader,

What a journey this book has been for me. When my editor called and asked me to write *Threat of Exposure,* book 5 in this series, I was thrilled. As is pretty typical of me, I just jumped right in and said I'd do it, not knowing what to expect. I didn't know anything about writing a continuity. However, I learned one thing pretty fast. It's HARD! But what a fabulous experience working with a group of authors I've read and admired for years. Trust me, it didn't happen overnight. I worked hard to get where I am today in the writing world. I've paid my dues, studied the craft, been rejected, pulled myself up and gone on to learn even more. *Threat of Exposure* is simply the result of all that hard work. In the same way, Gisella, armed with the skills she'd been trained in, jumped at the opportunity to go to Boot Hill, Texas, to fight for justice. She was determined to find her captain's killer and capture those who seek to harm people. Of course, Gisella had her issues, as did Brock, but together they worked through them, trusting God to lead them to make the right choices. In the end, they made the choice to conquer fear and love each other. Which, in my opinion, is always the right choice.

As always, I love to hear from readers. My email is lynetteeason@lynetteeason.com and my website is www.lynetteeason.com. You can also sign up for my newsletter here if you're interested in keeping up with new releases and contests. I'm also a regular blogger (as are all the authors involved in this series) at www.ladiesofsuspense.blogspot.com, where we talk about writing books, God and life—and not necessarily in that order. We also give away books on a regular basis. Please stop by anytime and feel free to bring a friend!

God Bless!

Lynette Eason

QUESTIONS FOR DISCUSSION

1. What do you think about Gisella? Do you like her? Why or why not?

2. What do you think about Brock? Do you like him? Why or why not?

3. Except for a brief time shortly after the death of her brother, Gisella remained strong in her faith. Brock was a believer, but God wasn't a priority in his life—until he was almost killed. Where are you in your faith? If God isn't a priority, what would it take to make Him one for you?

4. What was your favorite scene in the book and why?

5. There is a scripture passage at the beginning of the story. Do you understand why the author chose it? Do you feel it's appropriate for the story? Why or why not?

6. We all have stress in our lives and we all deal with it in our own way. Gisella chose a physical outlet: swimming. Not only was it good exercise, but it was a way for her to feel close to God. She prayed as she swam. What do you do

to deal with the stress in your life? What makes you feel close to God?

7. Gisella wanted to mend the strained relationship she had with her parents. At least she said she did and yet, she avoided going home and didn't answer their calls unless she absolutely had to. Thankfully, she finally realized those actions weren't going to do it. She had to get proactive about communicating with her parents. Is there someone in your life you need to get proactive about communicating with in order to heal the relationship?

8. Brock had seen his friend, Paul, love and lose someone Paul worked with. This made Brock extremely skittish about getting close to Gisella. But he couldn't seem to help himself. When he almost lost her, he had to make a choice. Overcome his fear and take a chance on a long life with the woman he loved—or lose her forever. He chose to take a chance. Is there something in your life you need to take a chance on or risk losing it forever? It may not even be another person. It could be a job, an opportunity, anything. What are the pros and cons of making that choice?

9. What do you think of Brock's willingness to be open and honest with Gisella about his feelings,

to be vulnerable to her? Did you like that or did you think it was a bit wimpy?

10. Gisella is a Texas Ranger, able to handle herself in pretty much any situation. After Brock saved her from almost drowning, she wanted to have a good cry. Did that make her seem weak to you? Or did you appreciate seeing the human side of her? The side that said, "I may be a Ranger, but I'm a woman, too."

11. Did the identity of the bad guy surprise you? Why or why not?

12. The topic of illegal aliens in the United States is a hot topic right now. How do you feel about those who are protecting our borders? Do you appreciate the job that they do? Why or why not?

13. Greed led Niles and the sheriff to be involved in smuggling drugs across the border. They were also guilty of several murders, including Ina and Jasper West. Do you think they could ever be forgiven for their actions? What does the Bible say about forgiveness?

14. These characters fell in love pretty quick. Is that believable to you? I knew I would marry the guy who is now my husband by our second date.

That was crazy for me! But I just knew! How about you? If you're married or engaged, at what point in your relationship did you realize you would marry that person?

15. Did you like the way the book ended? Why or why not?

LARGER-PRINT BOOKS!

GET 2 FREE
LARGER-PRINT NOVELS
PLUS 2 FREE
MYSTERY GIFTS

Love Inspired®
SUSPENSE
RIVETING INSPIRATIONAL ROMANCE

Larger-print novels are now available...

YES! Please send me 2 FREE LARGER-PRINT Love Inspired® Suspense novels and my 2 FREE mystery gifts (gifts are worth about $10). After receiving them, if I don't wish to receive any more books, I can return the shipping statement marked "cancel". If I don't cancel, I will receive 4 brand-new novels every month and be billed just $4.74 per book in the U.S. or $5.24 per book in Canada. That's a saving of at least 24% off the cover price. It's quite a bargain! Shipping and handling is just 50¢ per book in the U.S. and 75¢ per book in Canada.* I understand that accepting the 2 free books and gifts places me under no obligation to buy anything. I can always return a shipment and cancel at any time. Even if I never buy another book, the two free books and gifts are mine to keep forever.

110/310 IDN FC7L

Name	(PLEASE PRINT)

Address	Apt. #

City	State/Prov.	Zip/Postal Code

Signature (if under 18, a parent or guardian must sign)

LARGER-PRINT BOOKS!

GET 2 FREE LARGER-PRINT NOVELS PLUS 2 FREE MYSTERY GIFTS

Larger-print novels are now available...